R

"Jake, how do you do that?" Toby whispered hoarsely as he moved his mouth to the soft, fragrant skin of her neck.

"Do what?" His hand had somehow slipped to her hips and was applying a subtle downward pressure as the muscles of his thighs thightened. His mind was flooded with memories of the way she'd looked the night they'd first kissed, the way she'd felt in his arms. He wanted to feel that again. He *had* to have that again.

"Make that crazy tingle?" she whispered. "When I was a child. . . ." She stopped speaking and caught her breath when his lips slid lower to follow the line of her delicate collarbone. "When I was a child my friends and I used to get a kick out of touching our tongues to flashlight batteries. This is the same thing. Only . . . only more, and deeper. . . ."

WHAT ARE *LOVESWEPT* ROMANCES?

They are stories of true romance and touching emotion. We believe those two very important ingredients are constants in our highly sensual and very believable stories in the *LOVESWEPT* line. Our goal is to give you, the reader, stories of consistently high quality that may sometimes make you laugh, sometimes make you cry, but are always fresh and creative and contain many delightful surprises within their pages.

Most romance fans read an enormous number of books. Those they truly love, they keep. Others may be traded with friends and soon forgotten. We hope that each *LOVESWEPT* romance will be a treasure—a "keeper." We will always try to publish

LOVE STORIES YOU'LL NEVER FORGET
BY AUTHORS YOU'LL ALWAYS REMEMBER

The Editors

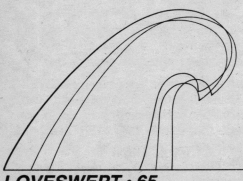

LOVESWEPT · 65

Billie Green
The Last Hero

BANTAM BOOKS
TORONTO · NEW YORK · LONDON · SYDNEY · AUCKLAND

THE LAST HERO
A Bantam Book / October 1984

LOVESWEPT and the wave device are trademarks of
Bantam Books, Inc.

ISBN 0-553-21673-2

Published simultaneously in the United States and Canada

PRINTED IN THE UNITED STATES OF AMERICA

O   0 9 8 7 6 5 4 3 2 1

One

Toby jerked her head up, and the movement sent the room spinning crazily around her. Inhaling slowly, she felt reality and the noise of the party and the people in the large room recede farther and farther from her lone figure on the elegant white sectional couch.

For a moment she struggled against the disoriented euphoria, then as the oscillating waves washed over her her eyelids drifted down and she gave in to the tingling, strangely erotic sensations. The curious vibrations attacking her nerve ends was something she had never experienced. A vague, almost disinterested smile touched her lips as she wondered what was happening to her. Then the remaining fragments of reality clashed head on with a spectacular, technicolored dream, and she was lost.

Toby slowly closed the door to her apartment behind her and leaned against it weakly, her breath coming in harsh, jerky gasps. Her key ring suddenly became too heavy for her trembling fingers, and when it fell to the floor she heard the noise as if it came from a great distance.

The slick sheen of perspiration covering her face and body was uncomfortable. Pushing away from the door, she walked unsteadily to the small, yellow bathroom adjoining her bedroom and reached into the stall to turn on the shower. Her clothes didn't seem to want to leave her body, and she was exhausted by the time she had removed them completely to step into the tiled enclosure.

The warm water slid over her skin, seeming to mingle with the sticky perspiration rather than wash it away. She picked up the tan bar of soap and began slowly to lather her flesh, but when the bar slipped away from her nerveless fingers, she left it on the tiled floor, too unsure of her movements to chance retrieving it.

As she rubbed away the remaining soap from her stomach and her thighs, she was plagued by a nagging sense that something wasn't quite right. Leaning against the wall, she tried to pinpoint the cause of her unease, but it kept sliding away from her before she could grasp it.

Moments later as she toweled herself dry she couldn't be sure how long she had stayed in the shower. Once again she seemed to have lost moments of her life to those waves of confusion.

She walked slowly to her bedroom and sat on the edge of her small, satin-covered bed. Picking up the phone, she glanced automatically at the old-fashioned copper alarm clock on the nightstand.

"Dr. Mathias," she murmured as the phone was picked up on the fourth ring. "Dr. Mathias, this is Toby. Something's wrong." She inhaled a shaky breath. "I'm having the weirdest dreams. I went back to high school . . . and I was naked. . . ." She gave a weak chuckle. "And nobody noticed. Then there was a room and an enormous bed . . . the biggest bed I've ever seen." Her words gained momentum as she spoke, and she couldn't get the words out fast enough as she continued in a breathless whisper. "It filled the room, with no space around it to walk . . . and there was a beautiful man . . . or the bronze statue of a man. I can't remember. Then there was a taxi and the driver had a nose like an aardvark—no, wait—it was Mr. Atkins, the vice-principal who had a nose like an aardvark, I think. Dr. Mathias—"

"Toby! Calm down."

Toby heard the doctor's voice, but it sounded distant and had the tinny quality of a transatlantic call.

"Listen to me, Toby. Did you pick up that prescription? Did you take the medication today?"

"Yes . . . yes, I think so. I took it just before I went to the party. What's wrong with me?" she whispered desperately. "Why were those children chasing me?"

"Toby, it wasn't real. You're having a reaction to the trifluoperazine that Dr. White and I prescribed for you."

Toby gave a hysterical laugh and leaned against the covered headboard. "You mean the drug you two gave me to keep me from going crazy made me go crazy? That's crazy."

"Stop it! Right now!"

The firm, quiet command reached her, and she drew in a deep, bracing breath.

"Now listen to me," the doctor continued. "Apparently the dosage was wrong for you. Confusion at night and bizarre dreams are a part of the reaction to too great a dosage. If I'm not mistaken the effects should be wearing off soon now, but you may have trouble sleeping and later there might be some changes in your menstrual cycle."

The doctor spoke in a soft, steady voice, as though she knew Toby wasn't taking in half of what she said, but was gaining confidence in hearing her speak.

"Go to bed now and try to get some sleep. If you feel the least bit strange later when you've been up awhile, call me. If not, I want you to come in Monday and we'll consult with Dr. White to find the correct dosage for this drug, or, if we decide you have an adverse reaction to it, we'll try something new. In the meantime don't take any more of the medication." She paused and Toby could hear the smile in her voice when she continued. "And Toby, if you see any more aardvarks in the next few hours, call me or Dr. White and we'll help you deal with them."

"If I see any more aardvarks, I may do more than call you," Toby muttered under her breath. "You may find yourself throwing a surprise slumber party."

The doctor's warm laugh steadied Toby and seemed to send the waves of confusion farther away.

"You're going to be just fine. I promise."

After mumbling good-bye, Toby replaced the receiver on the hook and pulled the towel from her damp hair. Already the weird dreams seemed to be fading from her memory. She sighed and closed her eyes. Thank heaven the strange night was over.

"Okay, Toby. You can get dressed. We're through."

Toby raised her head to give Dr. Mathias a quizzical glance over her sheet-draped knees. *"We're through? I didn't do anything . . . unless you* count the time I screamed when you used that refrigerated shoe spoon."

Dr. Mathias laughed softly, and the wrinkles around her hazel eyes deepened. "Okay, *I'm* through then," she corrected.

Suddenly her eyes narrowed and she stared thoughtfully at Toby for a moment, then she turned away and began to fuss with some instruments that lay on the gleaming white counter. After a moment she seemed to come to a decision. Turning around, she leaned against the counter and glanced over to where Toby was sitting on the edge of the examination table with the sheet pulled around her like a pale green sarong.

The laugh lines around the older woman's eyes relaxed, her features becoming somber as she continued to stare at her young patient with worried eyes. "Toby, I'd like to see you in my office when you're dressed," she said, her voice softly feminine, but firm.

Although Toby hadn't seen Dr. Mathias since the Monday after that weird weekend three months ago, she had known her for nine years, and never once during those years had she heard her use that tone of voice. It raised goose flesh on Toby's arms.

Swallowing nervously, she nodded, then sat silently as she watched the older woman leave the small examining room.

When the door closed softly behind the doctor, Toby shook her head in confusion, and short, chocolate-brown curls bounced around her head as though they had suddenly taken on a life all their own.

Crawling awkwardly off the table, she began to dress, wondering about the meaning behind Dr. Mathias's strange tone. Considering where she was and the routine yearly gynecological examination she'd just had, the possibilities seemed endless.

I'm sorry, Toby, but you only have thirteen weeks to live, and since you're going to die anyway the government of the United States would like you to blow up the Kremlin.

Giving her head a sharp shake, she tried to concentrate on getting her clothes on, but somehow managed to pull on the cream V-neck sweater backward. Without pausing she drew in her arms and turned the sweater around. Her eyes were dazed and dreamy as she stared straight ahead.

I'm sorry, Toby, but I have to tell you that you have a family of teeny, tiny people living in your uterus, and they're demanding that you redecorate the place.

But that image was too much even for her vivid imagination, and her thoughtful mood was destroyed by giggles. Even though she dressed more slowly than usual, taking time to run an unnecessary comb through her hair, still the minutes ticked by too fast. Finally, after picking several pieces of lint off her violet wool slacks, she knew she could no longer put off the inevitable, and grabbing her purse she made her way to the doctor's office.

She knocked softly when she reached the white door with Dr. Mathias's plaque on it.

"Sit down, Toby," the doctor said as she entered. "And stop looking so scared."

Toby noticed ruefully that she didn't say there wasn't anything to be afraid of, just in effect "don't look like there is." Suddenly her dark brown eyes widened as a new thought struck her. She had forgotten all about the drug that Dr. Mathias and Dr. White had decided she should take briefly for anxiety and depression. Aah, the devious little capsule that had caused such problems for her on that weird night. It had to be that. Toby's reaction to the drug had been too violent. Maybe an irregular menstrual cycle and the wild dreams weren't the only side effects of the drug. Perhaps it had done permanent damage. Maybe it had brought on a disease that was new and deadly and had no treatment. Maybe . . .

"Toby! I told you not to worry about it," Dr. Mathias said, removing her glasses to give Toby a stern look.

"But *you're* worried," she accused. "I can tell. Does it have anything to do with that stuff I took? That tri-whatever-you-call-it?"

Dr. Mathias didn't answer right away as though she were measuring her words. "There were no lasting effects from the overdose, no. You needn't worry about the effect of that episode on your . . . er . . . health."

Toby sighed in relief, then as she took in the older woman's frown her relief fled. "But there's something, isn't there? Something bad." She leaned forward suddenly, her vivid imagination taking over once again. "Don't nuns get cervical cancer from never having intercourse? Is that it? Am I going to die because I'm a virgin at twenty-three when everyone else starts sleeping around before they're weaned?"

"A virgin," the doctor murmured, giving her a thoughtful look. "Actually, that's what I wanted to talk to you about," she said slowly. She glanced down as she reached into her drawer, then leaned across her desk to hand Toby a small bag of peanuts.

Toby looked down at the peanuts in her hand, and suddenly her heart began to pound. "It's got to be something awful if I'm going to need peanuts," she whispered, her eyes growing large in her small, delicate face.

"There's no easy way to tell you this," the doctor said quietly, then she sighed heavily and placed both her arms on her desk to lean closer. "Toby, you're not a virgin."

"Well, no, not technically because of that accident when I was ten. But hymen or no, I'm a vir—" She stopped abruptly as she saw the look in the doctor's eyes. "No?" she said, her eyes puzzled.

Dr. Mathias shook her head in a cautious negative motion, still watching her closely.

"But how could you know that unless . . ." Her eyes widened and she tore open the peanuts. "Pregnant?" Toby whispered in a hoarse squeak.

The doctor's blue eyes went soft with feeling as she nodded.

"But that can't happen," she gasped. "I mean, every teenager has heard stories about getting pregnant from the water in a public pool, but it doesn't happen . . . does it?"

"I'm afraid not," she said softly, shaking her head again. Then she sighed as Toby turned the bag of peanuts up and took half of them into her mouth.

Toby's eyelids drifted down as the truth sank in slowly.

Guess what, Toby, you've been chosen to do a remake of Rosemary's Baby.

"A tumor!" Toby said suddenly, her eyes brightening as she sagged back in the chair and swallowed the peanuts heavily, then she laughed. "That happens all the time." She glanced at the gray-haired woman hopefully.

But Dr. Mathias didn't give her time to pursue that false line of reasoning. "It happens, but not with you, Toby." She hesitated, leaning back in her chair to stare at the ceiling for a moment. When she spoke, her voice was cautious. "You said you went to a party just before your . . . your confusion three months ago. Tell me about that."

Toby pressed her hands tightly to her stomach. "You think I . . . but I wouldn't have . . . Dr. Mathias, you know I wouldn't—"

"Tell me about the party, Toby."

"I can't tell you anything," she said, shaking her head in confusion. "I took a capsule about half an hour before Lynda and I left for the party. I remember arriving. I didn't drink because you told me not to—then I can't remember anything else. Lynda said I wouldn't leave when she wanted to." She paused and drew in a deep breath. "The next thing I remember clearly is telephoning you. I can vaguely recall coming home. And I think I took a shower. But that's all." She paused, her brow wrinkling as she searched her memory in confusion. "It was five in the morning when I finished talking to you, so I must have lost about six hours." She gave a shaky laugh of disbelief. "You're saying that sometime in those six hours I . . ." Her voice faded and her eyes darted around the room for a sign that what was happening to her was real.

"You can say it, Toby," the doctor murmured. "You can't think of it as a personal failing. There's nothing for you to be ashamed of." She paused and looked Toby straight in the eye. "During those hours that you can't remember, you made love."

Toby emptied the bag of peanuts in her mouth as the room began to spin about her.

There's nothing to be ashamed of. Don't think of it as being schizophrenic. Think of it as never having to watch a funny movie alone.

"How do you feel about it?"

She jerked her head up as the doctor's softly spoken words penetrated the solid wall of her reflections. She rubbed her chin and stared at the older woman thoughtfully for a moment, then she shook her head slowly. "About being pregnant?" Toby hedged warily.

"You know what I'm talking about," Dr. Mathias chided. "About being that close to a man."

"I don't know. I don't have that feeling in my stomach like I usually do. Maybe because I can't remember what happened. It's like when I watch a sexy movie. It doesn't bother me because I'm removed from it." She paused, trying to gauge her own reactions as she always did in a new situation. "It's funny, but the only thing I feel about that part is frustration."

"Frustration?"

"Yes, it's probably the only time in my life that I'll sleep with a man . . . and I missed it."

Dr. Mathias laughed. "I love the way you look at things, Toby."

Toby tilted her head to the side and gave a crooked, wry smile.

You're a mental case, Toby. A bag of neurotic tricks. But by golly, you're fun to have around.

"But really, you shouldn't think of it as an end," Dr. Mathias continued, her voice taking on a strange excitement. "It may be a beginning for you. A blessing in disguise."

"You think so, huh?"

It's too bad about having your arm amputated, Toby, but just think how much money you'll save on soap.

"There's something else we need to talk about, Toby."

"There's more?" she said warily. "But I'm out of peanuts."

Dr. Mathias laughed again. "I'm hoping you

won't need them for this. It's about the pregnancy. Before you can make a decision, there are some things you need to know purely from the medical point of view. First, the drug wouldn't have had an effect on the fetus. It should be normal. We can do some tests to make sure, however. Second, you're in excellent physical condition and you should have a normal healthy pregnancy. So the decision for you isn't a medical one, Toby. It's moral. It's emotional. It's purely personal. What do you want to do about it?"

Toby looked down at her hands. Dr. Mathias had tactfully avoided using the word "baby" throughout her little speech. She knew the woman was asking her whether she wanted to terminate the pregnancy. What *did* she want to do about it?

"I don't know, Dr. Mathias," she said slowly. "It's something I'll have to think about. You know I've always been vehemently pro-life, but . . . well, it's hard to be objective when it's come as a surprise like *this*." She shook her head. "I'll have to think about it." Her voice dropped to a whisper. "It's hard to believe that there's a baby growing inside me."

Baby. She should never have said the word aloud. It made it more real. It made abortion impossible to consider.

"Let me . . . let me think it over for a while. How far along am I?" Then she gave a rueful laugh. "That was a dumb question. The party was three months ago so I must be three months along."

"Yes, but there's still time if you decide soon." Dr. Mathias stood, indicating it was time for her next appointment. "You go home and think about it, Toby."

He stood in the dark, his heart pounding as he thought of the miracle that had just taken place.

Reaching out, he pulled back the drapes so he could see her better as she lay naked amid the rumpled covers on his large bed.

It was strange, but except for her urgent whispers during their lovemaking he didn't think he had heard her say a word. But then he hadn't spoken either. Words hadn't seemed necessary between them.

He had known when he took her in his arms to dance that it was right. There was something primitive in him that reached out to a similar chord in this small, sensual woman. And when the record ended, his arm had stayed around her waist, then—as though they had come to a silent agreement as they danced—they walked together out the door and away from the noisy, crowded party.

He smiled ruefully when he thought of how he had balked at the idea of going to the party. He hadn't been in the mood for people, but he had known how disappointed Ron would be if he didn't show up.

Now he thanked whatever kind fate had urged him to go. If he hadn't, he wouldn't have met her. And it was the first time in years that he had felt he was really making love instead of simply going through the motions. Even after he had escaped his disastrous marriage, his affairs had lacked the spark of feeling he had been unconsciously searching for.

As he stood silently watching her, her eyes flickered open. She ran a hand through her short, chocolate curls, then she saw him standing in the pale moonlight and smiled.

Slowly he began walking toward her. . . .

Toby sat in the living room of her apartment and

began to chuckle as she recalled the doctor's words, then the chuckle grew to laughter.

"Think about it," Dr. Mathias had said. As though she had a choice. As though she could think of anything else. Ever since she'd left the doctor's office she had thought of nothing else. She was still confused and frightened, but of one thing she was sure. Abortion was out.

She had read all the literature on the subject—the pros and the cons. She agreed that she owned her body. But she owned her car too. That didn't give her the right to drive it into a river if there was a passenger inside. Maybe it wasn't convenient, but should a life be looked at in terms of convenience?

So slowly Toby had come to accept the fact that she really was going to have a baby. And slowly she came to view the fact as a wonderful surprise, an early birthday present. A baby was something Toby had never considered possible for herself. She had been sure that she was destined to spend her life alone. But now without trauma, with no effort on her part, she had the miracle inside her.

She accepted this new turn of events as she always had accepted the strange curves life was constantly hurling at her. Once the fact that the situation was real had sunk in, she moved on to how she was going to handle the reality, wasting no time worrying over the "whys" and "if onlys."

After all it wasn't the first time she had had to adjust to an uncomfortable situation, she thought, giving a twisted smile. Her life seemed to have been filled with uncomfortable situations.

As a child she had arranged her life around the cold formality with which she was treated by her parents, never pining for the warmth that they were incapable of giving her. And she had slowly, painfully adjusted to the death of her dearly loved younger brother.

Then when she was eighteen and found out just how much her presence interfered in her parents' lives, she hadn't thought twice about moving out and starting her own life. And when she realized that the only members of the opposite sex who didn't make her stomach churn and her palms sweat when she was close to them were either teenagers or elderly men, she had learned to manipulate situations to suit her problems.

She had faced the debilitating periods of depression with a calm acceptance and simply went about trying to handle them rather than giving in to what she considered the darkness in her soul.

She had seen dream after dream trampled in the dust . . . and she had survived with only hairline fractures to her heart and an almost negligible loss of sanity.

She grinned suddenly. After all that having a baby was a piece of cake. Suddenly an unexpected joy began to well up inside her. She would give this baby all the love, all the care that had been so noticeably absent in her own life. Yes, she thought, this baby would be very much loved.

The only thing that really worried Toby now was the father of her child. Who was he? What was he like? After all her baby was going to inherit his genes too.

She frowned suddenly. Suppose he was criminally insane? What if his ears stuck out or he bit his nails? What if he was funny looking?

Yes, darling. Mother knows it's a problem, but I'm sure if you'll comb your hair to the side your little pointed head won't be nearly as noticeable.

She shook her head. It wasn't important. She would love it no matter what it looked like. But that didn't keep curiosity from driving her crazy. Somehow she couldn't associate the fact that she was pregnant with a man. Logically she knew one had to be involved, but since she had met him in the confusion of her lost weekend, she couldn't believe in his existence.

How would this man—whoever he was—react to the fact that he was going to be a father? Although she would never tell him, even if she knew who he was, she couldn't help but wonder about his reaction. Was he kind? Sensitive? Would her child inherit those qualities?

She frowned as an uncomfortable thought occurred to her. Did she have the right to keep this from the unknown father of her child?

She'd grown up with the cold manipulation of her parents, and she knew how harmful that could be. Somehow she couldn't picture herself doing the same thing. Could she do it without being haunted by it for the rest of her life?

Suddenly her frowning concentration was broken abruptly when the doorbell rang.

"Lynda!" she exclaimed when she saw her friend standing in the hall outside her front door. "You're just the person I want to see." Grabbing the plump blond girl's arm she pulled her into the living room.

"Well, I'm glad to see you, too." Lynda laughed as she dropped to Toby's yellow overstuffed sofa. "But maybe not so *violently* glad."

Toby couldn't manage to summon up her usual grin. Too much had happened to her, was still happening to her today. She sat in the huge green armchair, drew her knees up, and wrapped her arms around them. "Lynda, tell me about the party."

At her friend's quizzical glance she continued.

"*The* party. The one I didn't want to go to, but under pressure went to anyway and passed out on my return from. That party."

"*That* party," her friend said, smothering a gleeful laugh. "What's to tell? It was given by one of the vice-presidents of SGC and—"

"No, not that stuff," Toby said, interrupting her impatiently. "You said I was so involved in talking with someone that I wouldn't leave when you did. Who?" she asked urgently. "Who was I talking to?"

"It was . . . oh, what is that twit's name? Harry, that's it!" She sat up straighter. "Harry Something-or-other. I couldn't understand why you wanted to stay to talk to Harry, 'The Eggplant that Bored Dallas to Death.' Since it was the first time I'd ever seen you that close to a member of the opposite sex who didn't either have acne or a hearing aid, I figured it was healthy. Even if he did happen to have the personality of last week's lasagna," she added maliciously.

Toby held up a slender hand to stop the flow of words. "This Harry Something-or-other, tell me about him."

"Toby, what's this all about? I can't believe you've suddenly developed a crush on *him*. He's not even a reasonable facsimile of a man. Somebody mushed out a copy in clay and stuck it behind one of the desks at the office. If you've finally decided to join the human race, can't you pick someone who at least bears a faint resemblance to a human?"

Not very reassuring, Toby thought, frowning. An ugly child she could accept, but a boring child?

"Toby?"

"I'm pregnant," she said, throwing out the words bluntly before sagging weakly in the chair. She sighed sadly. "And apparently Gumby is the father."

Toby began rubbing her chin thoughtfully while she gave Lynda time to go through apoplexy. When her friend's face toned down to a bright pink and her breathing was just faintly raspy, she continued. "Lynda, I want to see him. Maybe he's not as bad as you say. Maybe his personality is the result of environmental rather than genetic factors."

"You're crazy," her friend muttered, staring at Toby with wide, dazed eyes.

Toby nodded vaguely. "What does that have to do with anything? I mean it! I want to see him. Why don't you ask him for dinner?"

"No way," Lynda said, shaking her head vehemently. "You don't know him. If I paid any attention to him at all I'd be stuck with him for the rest of my life." She hesitated. "Toby, did you really . . ." Her voice drifted off as though she couldn't say the words.

"Apparently I did." She closed her eyes briefly, then took a deep breath and continued. "And I've got to see him. There's something else I've thought about today." She paused, searching for the right words. "When I first thought of the father, I wanted it to stay the way it is now. I just didn't want to know." She sighed. "Then I started thinking about how I would feel if I were the father." She turned to look at her friend. "Lynda, I would want to know. I can't assume automatically this man is the type of person who could shrug off being a father. I would hate it if someone kept that kind of knowledge from me."

"If they kept it from you, you wouldn't know about it and it wouldn't worry you," Lynda said.

"I know. It doesn't make sense. But no one has the right to make decisions for another person.

You know how I feel about manipulation. If he doesn't want to know, then I'll tell him I made a mistake." She ran a distracted hand through her short curls. "Oh, I don't know." She groaned. "I'm confused. I don't *want* to confront this Harry, but somehow I feel that I've got to. Maybe when I talk to him I'll be able to get some clue to his personality. Maybe I won't have to tell him."

A stubborn glint in her eye, she looked at Lynda. "But first I have to talk to him. And I want you to help me arrange it."

Lynda must have recognized the determination in her friend's face for she sighed and nodded. "All right, if you really feel that strongly about seeing him, come have lunch with me tomorrow. He always eats in the company cafeteria." She paused. "But I have a feeling you're going to be sorry."

"Mr. Hammond."

Jake looked up with dazed eyes to see his secretary just inside his office door.

"Excuse me, sir, but you didn't answer your buzz. Mr. Ionesco is on line one. Do you have time to talk to him?"

"I'm sorry, Doris." He shook his head to clear it. "Yes, I'll talk to him."

Seeing the puzzled look his secretary gave him before she closed the door, he gave a short laugh. He was really too old for daydreaming, he told himself.

It had been three months since the party. Three months since the mysterious woman who had touched him for a such a brief time had walked out while he was in the shower. No note. No good-bye. Nothing but a rumpled bed to show that she had been there. No, that wasn't quite true. She had left something behind. Something inside him. A cleansing. A renewal. And wherever she was, who-ever she was, he silently thanked her.

Toby took a bite of the rubbery green gelatin salad and surreptitiously glanced around the small, bright cafeteria. "Why isn't he here?" she whispered to Lynda without turning to look at her. "I thought you said he had lunch here every day."

"He does. Don't worry, he'll be here. The whole building would collapse if he ever deviated from his set pattern," Lynda muttered, then paused thoughtfully. "Toby, are you sure you want to do this? I really think you would be better off not knowing what he's like. It would prejudice you against the baby before it even gets here to make its own impressions."

Toby chuckled at the wariness in her friend's voice. "Nothing can do that." She glanced at Lynda, then away again as she added thoughtfully, "I think I just want to convince myself that it really happened. Somehow I can accept the baby, but not that I"—she gulped nervously, then hurriedly took another bite of her salad—"that I slept with a man."

"It'll be even harder for you to believe when you see him," Lynda muttered dryly. "I really think you're going to regret this."

Toby shrugged. "It won't be the first time I've done something I've regretted. Besides I talked to Janine White last night, and she told me I should do this."

"When have you ever listened to your analyst?" Lynda said indignantly. "Remember the time she told you—" Suddenly she broke off and became perfectly still, her eyes narrowing. "That's him," she hissed, grasping Toby's arm urgently.

Toby didn't know what she had expected, but it

certainly wasn't the reality. Standing in line, pushing his tray along the rail, was a thin man of average height. His straight sandy-blond hair fell forward onto his forehead, and he walked in what appeared to be a permanently stooped position.

"He's not that bad," Toby said doubtfully. "At least he's not too short. Maybe the baby won't be a shrimp."

"Not that bad?" Lynda was astonished. "Toby, he's a weiner. I don't mean his looks. This is not first-generation dullness. It had to have taken several centuries of breeding to make him as boring as he is."

"I love the way you always try to look on the bright side," Toby muttered, then drew in a deep breath. "I'm going to talk to him."

Before her friend could protest, she stood and walked across the room to where he was placing his tray on an empty table.

"Hi."

The blond man glanced up at her and stared quizzically for a moment, then she could see by the recognition in his pale gray eyes that he had placed her. "Hi," he said slowly, then frowned as though suddenly faced with a problem. "I only have a few minutes. Did you . . . did you want to sit down?"

"Yes, I'd like to talk to you," she said, keeping her voice firm. She pulled out a chair, then added, "But you can go ahead and eat."

She waited while he removed all the dishes from his tray, arranged them precisely, then took several minutes trying to find a way to dispose of his tray.

"You said you wanted to talk to me about something?" he said finally, frowning and taking a bite from his sandwich.

"Yes." Toby drew in a deep breath before

continuing. "Actually it's about the party where I met you and . . . and everything."

He continued eating without looking up again, and she began to feel extremely uncomfortable. How could she approach the subject?

"Harry, I'm having a problem remembering the night we met." She laughed nervously and felt as though the laugh caught in her throat. "You see I was on medication and it had some . . . side effects." There was still no reaction from him. He simply continued to eat. Pressing her hands to her stomach, she lifted her chin in determination. "Apparently you and I . . . that is . . . we got along well."

"Yes." He sipped noisily through a straw pushed at a tilt into a carton of milk. "Yes, I think you could say that. Of course, being strangers, you couldn't really say we became friends. Friends develop over the years . . . or not, as the case may be. Don't you think? But as for enjoying the one night, I think we had an enjoyable evening."

Did Lynda say boring? Toby's eyes were already drooping when he finally got to the part that interested her.

"At least the first part of it was," he continued, scooping potato salad into his mouth. "I'm still not too happy about the last part, but really when two people don't know each other well you can't expect everything to go smoothly."

"You didn't enjoy the . . . last part?" she murmured weakly.

"No, not at all. I mean, when you've done it once what else is there?" His voice took on a faint, whining quality. "I really can't see why people enjoy it so much."

Oh, God! Her poor child had Gumby for a father.

Gumby with a nasal whine. She swallowed heavily. "I'm sorry you didn't enjoy it. Was it my fault?"

"Really I can only put part of the blame on you." He looked up at last. "I guess you could say it was my own fault. I'm too intelligent to enjoy anything that . . . physical."

She shouldn't have come to find him, Toby realized suddenly. There was no way this man would want to know about her pregnancy. She could just hear him trying to whine his way out of it.

"Of course if you had stayed at the party I might have enjoyed the last part more."

She gasped, giving him a stunned look. "Wait! What are you talking about?"

"Charades. After you left we played charades, and I just can't get into those silly games. I've always felt any truly sensitive person would have trouble understanding the point of . . ."

Her eyes closed as she went weak with relief. She hadn't left the party with mushed clay. She hadn't made love to him, and he wasn't the father of her baby!

"Speak of the devil," the blond man murmured, apparently unaware of the gift he had handed her.

Toby looked up and followed his gaze to a man who was carrying his tray to a table across the room. He was tall and solidly built, but walked with a strangely graceful stride, his beautifully tailored brown suit fitting his muscular body like a sleek second skin. His brown hair was streaked with gold and curled slightly, reminding her of a Greek god that had been forced to adjust to the modern world.

Suddenly the room dissolved around her and she saw before her a bronzed statue, sleek and strong, the smooth lines gleaming in soft light. Where had she seen it? And why was the memory so vivid?

She shook her head in confusion and watched as he slid into the booth across the cafeteria. He raised his head for a moment, and she saw the brilliant blue eyes rake the room, then return to the tray before him.

Only when she exhaled painfully did she realize she had been holding her breath. Never in all her twenty-three years had she been so deeply affected by the mere sight of another human being. It was unbelievable and totally unexplainable.

As Toby stared, she suddenly felt a strange sensation spread through her body. Without knowing a thing about him, she could physically feel his hard male strength and his keen intelligence. It was the strangest feeling, as though for a moment she had reached inside a man she had never seen. A man who had nothing whatever to do with her life.

Running her hand slowly across her face, she felt an echo of the disorientation she had experienced on that night three months ago. The peculiar effect this stranger had on her wasn't a sensation she was comfortable with, and she fought to shake it away and return her thoughts to the blond man beside her who had begun to speak again.

"I suppose we should feel honored that Mr. Bigshot Hammond himself is having lunch with us lesser beings today." Harry's voice was filled with malice. "I never could understand why you left the party with him, but I suppose I shouldn't have been surprised."

Harry paused and smiled in a knowing way that sent unpleasant shivers down Toby's spine. "After all why should you spend time with a junior accountant when you can have the boss?"

Two

Toby sat with her lower lip drooping slightly in an unconsciously sensual pout, and her heart began to pound in crazy skipping beats. Then she stood abruptly and walked away, leaving Harry to stare indignantly after her for a moment before shrugging and continuing with his lunch.

She sat down in her former seat beside Lynda, thankful that her legs had not collapsed beneath her on the short walk. For several moments she felt she couldn't speak if her life depended on it.

"Well, what did he say?" Lynda whispered urgently, leaning closer. "Did you tell him about—"

"Lynda," she interrupted, unaware that her friend had even spoken. "Who is that?" She cut her eyes toward the man in the corner of the room without moving her head.

The blonde frowned impatiently, then, taking in her friend's dazed expression, she glanced over her shoulder. "That's Mr. Hammond. Jacob Hammond."

"I know that much, but who is he?" Toby rubbed her chin nervously with the palm of her hand as she waited anxiously for Lynda's reply.

"He's one of the vice-presidents. I forget which," Lynda murmured, her expression revealing her growing concern as she watched Toby.

"Oh." Toby's mouth retained the shape of the word as she stared at him. Somehow it had seemed easier when she thought the father of her child was an ordinary man. She didn't know if she could approach *this* man.

"One of the top cats," Lynda continued. "They say he'll be running the place in a few years. Some say that secretly he's doing it now." She stared thoughtfully at the man in question, then switched her eyes back to her friend. "Toby, what's going on? Why are you so interested in him?"

Toby stared down at her hands, which were clasped tightly together on the table, then slowly looked up at Lynda and smiled wistfully.

"Toby," the blonde gasped, her eyes widening in shock. "Him?"

"Uh-hum," she murmured, watching as another man stopped beside his table to talk to him briefly. "Him." She inhaled deeply. He rose and made his way through the crowded cafeteria. "Lynda, do you know anything about him personally?"

"Only what I've heard from the gossips," Lynda said, her voice faint. "Are you sure? What did Harry say?"

"He said I left the party with Hammond," she said, then shook her head to clear it. "Tell me, Lynda, tell me anything . . . even the gossip."

"He's in his early thirties," she began, her voice vague with shock, then she shook her head and continued. "I think he's been with the company for about eight years. Apparently Hammond is a sharp businessman because even my boss has a touch of awe in his voice when he talks about him." She leaned forward to rest her chin on her hand thoughtfully. "He's been divorced for two years, was married for five. I've seen his ex-wife. She's a gorgeous brunette who always seems to have a fur draped around her."

"Does he have children?"

"No. At least not by her. She just had a baby by her new husband. She brought it with her last time she came to see him." She shrugged. "I thought it seemed a little strange, but I figured they had one of those friendly divorces and she was showing off the baby."

"So he's intelligent and ambitious. Anything else?"

"Well, there's usually gossip about some woman or other that he's interested in here at the company, but I think it's just gossip. He's the natural target for that stuff — single, good-looking, and in a high position — so you can't put much stock in it. I've never even spoken to him, and I can't say what he's like personally. I just know that nobody ever talks about what a nice guy he is, only what a great businessman he is." She paused and grinned maliciously. "And the people who have come to his attention because they screwed up on their jobs hate him with a passion."

That wasn't exactly comforting. Toby chewed her lip for a moment. She couldn't make a decision based on gossip. She had to meet the man himself. She couldn't stop just because he was important instead of ordinary.

"Toby," Lynda said hesitantly. "What are you going to do now?"

She shrugged. "Somehow I have to find out if he's the one. When you told me about Harry, I thought I only needed to find out if he should know about the baby or not. But now, everything's crazy. I know it wasn't Harry, but I'm still not positive it was Hammond. I could have left him after we walked out of the party." She shook her head in confusion. "I don't know what to think. I guess I'll have to go see him."

Then she remembered the decisions she had made the day before, and suddenly, as though someone infinitely stronger were in control of her mind, her decision was made. "I'm going to see him now. And if I can't get in to see him, then maybe I'll know that it's the wrong move." She shivered as she remembered the sternness of his outstandingly attractive features, and some of her strength seeped away. "If I can get in, then I'll decide what to tell him when I see him."

She paused, giving her friend a worried glance. "Oh, how I wish he were a little more ordinary . . . a little less overpowering. I always become incoherent around that kind of man."

"Don't think of him that way," Lynda said, resting her forearms on the table. "Anytime I feel intimidated by someone—like Mrs. Jones in the credit union—I just imagine that they're sitting there with no clothes on." She chuckled and her eyes twinkled with mischief. "Picture what she'd look like naked! It always works. All of a sudden they seem ordinary . . . even ridiculous. You can't be afraid of someone who looks ridiculous." She paused and took in Toby's skeptical expression. "I promise you it will work."

Toby kept her eyes trained on the neat, efficient secretary sitting behind the desk across the room from her, but her thoughts weren't on the attractive redhead. They were wholly, completely on the man in the next room.

Surprisingly she had no trouble in obtaining a last-minute appointment with Jacob Hammond. She had explained to the secretary that it was important and personal. After the woman made a quick call, staring strangely at Toby as she answered questions put to her by her employer, she nodded and told her Mr. Hammond would see her.

Now that she knew he would see her she couldn't decide what on earth she could say when she got into his office. Even if she could manage to discipline her emotions so she wouldn't be intimidated by him, what was she going to say to him? There should be a discreet way of bringing up the subject of the night they spent together, but if there was, Toby certainly couldn't find it. She had practiced leading statements over and over in her mind, but they still sounded impossible.

"Ms. Baxter?"

Toby jerked her head up and saw the secretary looking at her expectantly.

"Mr. Hammond will see you now."

Toby swallowed a nervous lump in her throat as the woman continued to stare at her. Slipping her hand in her purse, she checked to make sure her peanuts were still there, then she stood, smoothed down the skirt of her paisley silk dress, and walked slowly to the large door on the far side of the room. She paused, stiffened her trembling muscles, then walked in, closing the door softly behind her.

The bright sunlight coming from the huge windows in the room blinded her for a moment, and she stopped just inside the door. Then she saw him. He was sitting at a large oak desk, his head bent over some papers. The sunlight streaming in through the windows clung to the golden streaks in his hair. She could see the lines carved deep into his brow as he concentrated intently on the papers lying on his desk.

He didn't look up as she walked forward, but indicated with a casual wave of his hand that she be seated in the suede chair facing his desk.

She waited patiently for the first few seconds, then the silence became too much for her nervous system and she began to fidget in the large, wingback chair.

Maybe this wasn't such a good idea after all. Maybe he believed that ignorance was bliss. Why should he care that a woman he barely knew was pregnant? Why should he care that the baby was his? Maybe he hated children. After all he had been married for five years and hadn't had any.

She eyed him warily as he continued slowly to sift through the papers. This was *not* the type of man who was usually referred to as a "good ole boy." This was a man who intimidated with a single glance.

Calm down, she told herself bracingly. *Don't think of him as a man. Think of him as a large teenager.*

But somehow she couldn't picture him as anything other than very much a man. Imagine him naked, Lynda had said. It's foolproof, Lynda had said.

Her eyes drifted over the part of his body that was visible above the desk. All she had to do was imagine him without the sleek brown jacket, without the soft blue shirt. Imagine his broad, tanned chest and muscular arms covered with curling golden hair. Imagine . . .

Oh Lord, she moaned silently, *wrong move*.

Reaching quickly into her purse, she pulled out the peanuts and began to rip open the package.

"Ms. Baxter."

The untimely recognition of Toby's presence jolted through her as though he had physically thrown the words at her and they'd hit the bull's-eye. Her body jerked in startled reaction to his deep voice—and the movement sent the peanuts flying.

She scrambled to scoop up the ones that had landed on the chair and in her lap, merely giving the ones on the floor a sorrowful glance. "I'm sorry," she said, shrugging apologetically. "You scared me."

Leaning back lazily in his high-backed leather chair, he simply continued to stare at her without saying a word.

Swallowing nervously, she clasped her hands together in her lap. "Mr. Hammond, I don't know if you remember me—"

"Yes, I remember you," he interrupted. He stared down at the pencil he held between his strong, tanned fingers. "In fact, I recognized you in the cafeteria. I'm just wondering why you didn't approach me there."

Bridge number one had been crossed. He remembered her. But what did he remember about her?

"I . . . I wanted to speak to you privately," she stuttered, unnerved by his unapproachable expression. She glanced up to find him waiting expectantly and cleared her throat. "It's about the party where we met."

She waited for a response, then when none was forthcoming she continued hesitantly. "Well, actually it's about what happened after the party."

"Ms. Baxter, I'm having a problem understanding why you're here." He leaned forward, his expression guarded, the depth of his blue eyes holding her immobile. "I remember that we met at Ron Ashley's party," he continued softly. "I also remember that we went to my house afterward." He lifted one heavy eyebrow. "Now where does that get us?"

Bridge number two. He had confirmed the fact that she had not only left the party with him but had gone to his house. There was no doubt this time. This was the father of her child. She sat studying him silently. A golden-haired baby? A tall child? Suddenly she frowned. A stern, intimidating child? She stared even more intently at his solid form. A healthy child?

Holding on to the arms of her chair, she said earnestly, "Mr. Hammond has there ever been any insanity in your family? Or inherited illnesses?"

Finally his smooth mask dropped away, and she watched with surprised fascination as his expression became lively for the first time since she had entered the room. He looked startled, and his features were aglow with curiosity. Before he had seemed an attractive man. Now he took her breath away.

"I beg your pardon?"

His voice was different as well. It contained genuine emotion. Even if the emotion was frustration or impatience, still it was recognizable emotion.

For a moment she thought she was going to be able to go through with it. He seemed so much more human, so much more approachable. Then she thought of the way his face would return to the grim lines when she told him that she was pregnant, and her courage deserted her completely.

She couldn't do it. Standing, she murmured,

"I'm sorry. I've changed my mind." Then she turned and walked to the door.

In the outer office, she nodded to the secretary and walked to the middle of the room, then hesitated. She couldn't leave now. Not until she confirmed the events of that night and made sure he wouldn't mind if she held back the knowledge that she was pregnant with his child. She had come here for a reason and couldn't just leave because he wasn't as helpful as she had wished.

Spinning around she walked back to his door and opened it to peek cautiously around the edge. He was still sitting, watching the door, just as though he had known she would return. Shrugging in resignation, her lips curved up in a small, brave smile, and she walked back to resume her former position.

"Mr. Hammond," she began briskly, "I took some new medication the night of the party, and I had a bad . . . a weird reaction to it." She hesitated, biting her lip, then clinched her fists and continued. "The truth is I don't remember meeting you that night. I don't remember anything that happened. And . . . and I would appreciate it very much if you would . . . well, fill me in on what happened. Without going into too great detail," she added hastily.

She wriggled uncomfortably when he tilted his chair back and stared at her silently for a long while. At last he began to speak, his deep voice sounding quiet and somehow dangerous.

"You don't remember?" Suddenly a wry smile twisted his lips, and Toby felt her heart skip a beat. In that brief moment she glimpsed a vulnerability in him that astonished her. She couldn't imagine any man, much less one as powerful and self-assured as this one, feeling vulnerable. Nevertheless she had definitely seen it. And it seemed as though she had been given this insight for a particular purpose. This man would care.

"I think what you're asking, Ms. . . . what's your first name?"

"Toby."

"Well, Toby, I think what you want to know is whether or not we made love."

She swallowed noisily and nodded.

"I can understand that." He smiled, and the change it made in his features had a mesmerizing effect on her, pinning her gaze to his firm, sensuous lips. "What I can't understand is why I get the feeling it's very important for you to know." He leaned forward in his chair suddenly and gave a short laugh. "But since it's really none of my business, I'll tell you anyway. Yes, we made love." He paused and smiled. "In fact, we made love several times. Does that help you?"

Help? She gulped silently. Oh, mercy! She had wanted the final confirmation, but never would she have believed that so few words could make such an immediate change in her body temperature and her pulse rate.

"Yes," she said breathlessly. "Yes, thank you. That's what I wanted to know." She hesitated, then closed her eyes and plunged in. "Why didn't you have children with your ex-wife?"

She heard him draw in a harsh, painful sounding breath, then there was silence. When it began to fill the room with an electric tension, she opened her eyes slowly.

His eyes were now closed, and harsh lines of unhappiness were etched deep in his face. Without thinking she blurted out, "I'm sorry. That's none of my business. It's just that I needed to know what kind of man you are and if you would even care." She moistened her lips nervously, aware that she had his complete attention now. "You might resent the fact that I told you about it. You might even consider it an inconvenience." She gave a shaky laugh. "It wasn't exactly something I expected myself. I mean, I don't even remember anything that happened, so you can imagine how surprised I was when I went for my regular checkup to be told that I'm three months pregnant."

She was so taken up by her own thoughts that she almost missed the expressions playing across his strong face. Then she groaned miserably when she realized what she had said.

Idiot! she castigated herself. What a way to tell him. She might as well have sent him a singing telegram. The shock on his strong face held her frozen in her chair. Then slowly the shock was replaced by a strange look of yearning, then dawning suspicion, and finally a black, frightening anger.

She stared silently at his clenched fists, then glanced up as he spoke. "You say you don't remember anything?"

Words wouldn't form in her throat. She sank deeper into the large chair and simply shook her head in a slight, negative motion.

"Then pardon me for being plain spoken," he said, his voice stiff with some dark emotion, "but how do you know I was the only man you slept with that night?"

She flinched at his bluntness, then slowly a look of blank astonishment crossed her expressive features. "You're right!" she said excitedly, stretching far forward in the chair. "I didn't even think of that. I have no way of knowing *what* happened."

The change in her that night had been so drastic, why shouldn't she assume it had been even more drastic? And if he needed a way out, she would be glad to provide it for him.

"Then you may not be the father after all," she whispered in amazement. She couldn't hide the relief in her voice. She stood up and smiled at him. "Never mind," she said brightly and walked out of the room, feeling several hundred pounds lighter.

She had taken only a couple of steps into the outer office when she felt her arm caught in an iron grasp. Silently and swiftly he jerked her back into his office and slammed the door behind her.

"You can't walk in here and drop that kind of bomb and then just excuse yourself with a 'never mind,'" he said, his voice grim. "I didn't say the baby isn't mine. I simply said I may not be the only candidate for its paternity."

He guided her back to the wingback chair, then glared at her until she sat down in a flustered heap. Turning away he ran his fingers through his hair, then swung around to direct his piercing stare at her. "What time did you get home that night?"

"I—" she began, then cleared her raspy throat. "I don't know. I think it was sometime between four and five in the morning."

For a moment he was strangely still, then he drew in a deep breath and she watched the fabric of his pale blue shirt stretch tight across his chest. "You left my house at four-thirty," he said in a monotone.

"Oh." She shifted in her chair, giving him a measuring glance beneath her long, dark lashes. "Then I'm afraid you're it."

She waited for a moment for some acknowledgment from him, then when he remained silent she began to feel that she should be trying to comfort him in some way.

"I'm sorry if that makes you uncomfortable," she murmured. "But you don't have to do anything about it. I only told you because I tried to imagine how I would feel if I were a man who had a baby that I didn't know about. I wouldn't like it. And of course, because Janine agreed with me that I should tell."

"Janine?" he said, giving her a dazed look.

"My analyst. She said I would feel guilty about keeping it from you. She also said that meeting you would make it seem more real and could even help me to remember. But it doesn't and it didn't. So there was really no need for me to trouble you."

She stood and wiped her hands on her skirt, then picked up her purse. "Was there anything else you wanted to know? If not, I have to go see Janine now. She wanted to get my reactions to our meeting." She paused and looked at him thoughtfully. "Could you do something unusual? She's always so disappointed when nothing unusual happens."

He stared at her for a moment as though she were a visitor from another world, then slowly his face changed and, incredibly, he began to laugh. The deep, rich sound drifted around the room, filling the remotest corner with a warmth she would never have associated with this man.

"I can't think of a single unusual thing right now," he said, still chuckling. "You're taking this very . . . casually, don't you think?"

She rubbed her chin with the palm of her hand. "I guess it would seem like it to you," she acknowledged. "But you have to remember I've had time to get used to it." She grinned irrepressibly. "Besides there never seems to be enough time to sit around and regret what's happening to me. All my time is taken up just coping. Now that I know that I really and truly am going to have a baby, there's so much to do," she finished, her voice fading away as her thoughts were claimed completely by her plans for the baby.

He had moved silently closer during her reflective speech and now he reached out and lifted her chin, forcing her to look up at him. "Toby Baxter, I think you must be the most extraordinary experience I've had in years," he murmured, his brown velvet voice sending strangely delicious shivers down her spine. "I thought so the night I met you, but today has definitely confirmed it."

Then it almost seemed that he sensed when his nearness began to make her feel uncomfortable, and without another word he stepped back and said briskly, "We need to talk more about this, Toby. I suppose you've already seen a doctor. A good doctor."

She nodded. "Dr. Mathias has been my doctor for nine years. She's the best."

"Good. Then I'd like to see you tonight." When he saw her frown he continued quickly, "We really do have things to talk about, Toby. You thought it was important that I know about your pregnancy . . . and it was. I can't just forget about it now."

She glanced at him, then away. "Yes, I guess you're right." She paused and looked up hopefully. "I could meet you somewhere."

He smiled the grim smile that was already becoming familiar to her. "This is not something we can talk over at MacDonald's. My house or yours?" he asked firmly.

Hearing the determination in his voice, she sighed heavily. "All right, make it mine. The Sunderland Apartments. Number four-fourteen." She quickly headed for the door.

"I'll be there at eight. And Toby . . ."

She stopped and glanced back at him over her shoulder.

"I'm the father of your child, remember? You really are going to have to stop jumping every time I come within two feet of you."

Three

Jake slid into his jacket, then eased his large frame onto the small chair that faced the cluttered desk of his longtime friend and personal physician, Mel Landers. Staring down silently at his polished boots, he waited for Mel to sit down before glancing up.

"So what you're saying is that while it's not very likely, it's possible," Jake said quietly.

His friend smiled wryly. "Actually I've carefully avoided saying anything at all. I'm just wondering what you want me to say, Jake."

"I want the truth. Nothing more and nothing less."

Mel leaned back in his chair and inhaled slowly. "All right. Here it is. The sperm count is still low. That hasn't changed, and I can't avoid the facts just because you want a child." He paused, pushing forward to rest his forearms on his desk, and added in a low, intense voice, "Jake, you simply cannot accept the word of any girl who walks in off the street."

"She's not just any girl. I made love to her, Mel. If you're interested in facts, that's one that can't be changed. And if there's even a slim chance that the child is mine, I can't ignore it." He stared at his friend's frowning face. "I know what you're thinking. You think she's after money." As Mel continued to stare at him silently, Jake moved restlessly in the narrow chair. "All right. I'll admit that it's a possibility, but somehow I can't believe she's after money. You'd have to meet her to know what I mean."

He laughed suddenly, remembering the peanuts still on his office floor. "She doesn't contain an ounce of artifice, Mel. It's not just that she's young. She's totally natural. You can't fake the kind of honesty I saw today."

He shrugged and pushed back in his chair when he saw Mel watching him with a strange look of comprehension that made him extremely uncomfortable.

"You're determined to accept this baby as yours, aren't you?" Mel asked, shaking his head. "Even though I've given you the facts and you've said the girl herself isn't sure what happened that night."

Jake nodded grimly, not liking the way his friend referred to Toby. "Her name is Toby, Mel. She's a person, not some slut who's trying to put one over on me."

"All right then: *Toby* is not really sure what happened that night," Mel amended. "Talk to her doctor, Jake. If Toby is telling the truth, it can't hurt. Make sure she's honest . . . and sane."

"Sane?"

"For all you know the girl may be sick. She may believe in something that isn't real." He stared down at his hands. "Find out what kind of person she is. You say she couldn't have been with anyone after you, but that doesn't mean she wasn't with a dozen men in the week before she met you." He paused and sighed as Jake glared at him angrily. "At least confirm the stage of her pregnancy. Who's her doctor?"

"Dr. Mathias."

Mel nodded. "She's a fine doctor. I would trust anything she told you." He stared down at his hands as Jake stood to leave. "And Jake . . ."

Jake paused, still frowning, and glanced down at Mel.

"Since you're determined to believe the baby is yours, maybe this will help." He pulled a medical journal out from under a stack of papers and handed it to Jake.

"What is it?"

"There's an article in there about fertility. Some new facts have come to light. Doctors are finding that the degree of excitement—the desire—felt by a couple may have something to do with fertility. Apparently increased desire raises the sperm count in men while the fluid secreted by the female makes her more receptive to the sperm." He gave Jake a look that was more curious than professional.

"And you're saying this might be true in my case?"

"Anything is possible," Mel said, smiling at the light growing in Jake's eyes. "If this applies to you, it simply makes the possibility more likely."

Slowly a smile spread across Jake's strong face as he thought again of the night he had spent with Toby, then he murmured, "If the degree of desire has anything to do with fertility, then it's more than just a possibility."

The waiting room of Dr. Mathias's small clinic was filled with plants and books and comfortable, non—waiting room—type furniture, reminding Jake of his great—aunt Sophie's parlor.

He stood with his back to the room, watching squirrels run up and down the ivy-covered tree outside the window, while he waited for his turn with the doctor.

When he had explained he was calling about Toby, the receptionist had put him right through to Dr. Mathias, who had seemed eager, even anxious, to fit him into her apparently busy schedule.

Jake wasn't pleased with the suspicions Mel had placed in his mind . . . and that worried him. The girl meant nothing to him. Why was he, Jacob Hammond the Cautious, so anxious to believe every word Toby said? Was it, as Mel had suggested, because he had all but given up on the prospect of ever being a father? Or was it something in Toby herself that pulled at him, making him want to believe she was as honest as she seemed?

Before he could get any further with the puzzle, the young receptionist called his name, then directed him to Dr. Mathias's office. He hadn't time even to be seated before a woman in her early fifties entered the room. Her gray hair was almost silver and matched the frames of the large, square glasses that rested low on her nose.

"Mr. Hammond," she said, extending her hand. "I'm very glad to meet you. I had no idea until you called that Toby intended to get in touch with you." She indicated the large tapestry-covered chair, then sat down behind the large desk that took up the corner of the room.

"She did, of course, call me last night to tell me

that she definitely wanted to keep the baby," she added.

Frowning, he half rose, then promptly settled back into the chair. "Was the alternative ever a possibility?"

Dr. Mathias smiled wryly. "With Toby? I'm afraid not."

"You're afraid?" he asked quizzically, feeling his heart skip a beat. "Will the pregnancy be dangerous for her?"

She removed her glasses and rubbed the bridge of her nose in what seemed more a habit than anything else. She seemed to be thinking over his question. At last she said, "Not physically. Mentally . . . I'm not sure." She grinned suddenly and lost five years in the process. "I have a hunch it may be just what she needs."

"I don't see what you mean, but then I don't understand anything about Toby." He hesitated momentarily. "You do realize that I had never met her before . . . before that night." When she nodded, he continued. "I need to learn more about Toby before I can decide what to do about the situation. I need to know what kind of person she is."

"And maybe you need to know that the baby is really yours," she suggested, smiling gently.

He moved uncomfortably in the chair. "The possibility exists, wouldn't you say?"

She stared steadily at him for a moment, then said, "Did Toby leave the party with anyone before she left with you?"

He frowned. "No, she didn't."

"Then there is no possibility," she said, her voice quietly firm. "Toby was a virgin before that night."

Her words hit him like a slap in the face, and he slumped back in the chair, reeling from the blow. "A vir . . . but she couldn't have been," he rasped out. "Look, doctor, that's not exactly something I would overlook. I'm not in the habit of making love to virgins."

He couldn't believe what this woman was telling him, then suddenly he remembered how young—how innocent—she had seemed today in his office. He had received a completely different impression than he had on that night three months ago. Then she had been all woman, seductive and mysterious, a dream he had not even known that he had dared to dream.

"Toby's been a patient of mine for a long time, Mr. Hammond," she continued, breaking into his confused thoughts. "And I know her much better than I know most of my patients." She laughed. "You can't be around Toby for very long without being totally captivated by her . . . um . . . unique personality."

She watched him assimilating her words for a moment, then continued. "She had an accident when she was ten that ruptured the hymen. But she had never had intercourse before that night with you. If you can accept my word, then I give you my word on that. I know Toby better than her own mother knows her, so this is not something I'm guessing about."

He sat silently for a moment sifting through the facts she had given him. There was so much to think about. He had come here to learn more about Toby Baxter, but he had never imagined how much there was to learn. Suddenly his thoughts switched away from the unbelievable fact of her virginity to something the doctor had said earlier.

"You said you weren't sure how the pregnancy would affect her mentally, and she told me she was seeing an analyst," he murmured thoughtfully. "Is there some problem? Or is she seeing an analyst simply because it's fashionable?"

The doctor pushed back in her chair and chuckled. "Toby never does anything because it's fashionable. In fact, she would go out of her way to do just the opposite. If you're asking if she's mentally disturbed, then the answer is no. She's probably more sane than ninety percent of the people walking the streets. And she has a way of dealing with her problems that's extraordinarily honest." She hesitated. "The fact is, she is still emotionally immature in some ways. I think having a baby will be a tremendous growing experience for her." She smiled. "If there's one thing you can be sure of, she'll throw herself into the pregnancy with complete abandon. She never does anything halfway."

Jake sighed in relief. "Then there's no problem with her raising a baby."

"No, no. Of course not." She shook her head vigorously. "I don't want to give you the wrong impression. It's simply that I can't go into the details of her problem without breaking a professional confidence, but believe me, it doesn't affect her rationality. I would trust Toby with my own grandchildren . . . and you can be sure she would protect them with her life. That's not what I meant by immaturity. She simply has problems dealing with her own emotions. . . . But then which of us doesn't?"

Jake thought again of that question later as he walked away from the clinic. "Which of us doesn't?" she had said. He thought of the personal problems that had overwhelmed him during his adult life. His dissolved marriage was a case in point. He felt he had badly mismanaged the whole affair. They had lost the ability to communicate somewhere along the way, and it had ended in bitterness.

The doctor was right. Not many people knew how to deal with their own emotions. But apparently Dr. Mathias thought Toby had a healthy attitude about her own. And she seemed extremely fond of Toby. That fact showed not only in what she said, but in her facial expressions when she talked about her. She was fond of Toby and she respected her. And Mel had said that Jake could trust the doctor's judgment.

At last Jake allowed the realization that he was going to be a father to penetrate. The confusion, the doubts, began to seep away to be replaced by a growing wonder and an almost painful joy.

Toby opened the door a fraction of an inch, then when she saw Jake standing there, she sighed, removed the chain, and opened it wide to let him in.

The tension had been building in her since their meeting that afternoon, and her meeting with Janine had done nothing to give her the confidence she needed in dealing with this man. More and more she was beginning to wish she had kept her mouth shut and simply pretended the baby had no father.

"How do you feel?"

His deep voice shook her out of her absorbing reverie, and she realized they were still standing in the center of the room.

"Sit down, Mr. Hammond," she murmured, indicating her brightly colored sofa. "I'm fine."

Toby, you silver-tongued devil, you're liable to intimidate him with such scintillating conversation.

He stared at her with a curious light in his striking blue eyes as he sat down. "Don't you think you'd better call me Jake?" At her hesitant nod, he rubbed his strong jaw, then said in determination, "And you're not having a problem with morning sickness?"

"No . . . Jake."

And now our award for putting the most people to sleep in the shortest amount of time goes to Toby Baxter.

"Toby!" he exploded in exasperation. "We need to talk."

What an excellent idea. Now why didn't I think of that?

She nodded slowly, still watching him closely as she sat across the coffee table from him in her favorite chair.

"I've done a lot of thinking since you left the office." He gave a rough laugh, leaning back against the overstuffed couch while he massaged the back of his neck. "You have to admit your visit was a little unusual. At first I thought about arranging some kind of account for you and the baby—"

"Account?" Toby said sharply. "You mean money? I don't need money. I've got a lot more than I'll ever use. That wasn't why I came to you. I just felt it was the right thing to do."

"Yes, I know that now," he said, his voice surprisingly soothing. "And even if you had come for money, I find that it's not enough for me."

She stared at him quizzically, her heart jerking to a halt, then resuming its normal function in a joltingly frantic beat. "Not enough?" she murmured warily.

He rose suddenly and walked across to where she sat, then when she moved deeper into the huge chair, he squatted beside her, grasping both her hands in his.

"Toby, you have to understand something," he said urgently, his eyes burning with a bright blue flame of intensity. "This could very well be the only child I ever have."

She swallowed the gravel in her throat to gasp, "But . . . but surely you'll marry again."

"Possibly," he acknowledged with a short nod. "But that doesn't matter. There are . . . reasons to believe that this is my only chance."

"Oh, I see." But she didn't see at all. And she couldn't get her brain to work long enough to try and figure it all out. She could only think of how close he was. How overwhelmingly close.

"So I don't want to miss any part of this child's birth," he continued, closely monitoring her reactions. "Including the time it spends inside your body."

Toby felt her bones dissolving into pure mush, and she wouldn't have been surprised to find herself oozing around on the chair like a beached jellyfish. She realized he hadn't intended what he said to sound personal. But it did. It sounded more than personal; it sounded incredibly intimate and she backed away from him mentally.

Think, Toby, she commanded silently. She had to think about what he was saying rather than the way it made her feel. He wanted to be included in the pregnancy. That was a reasonable request, she assured herself.

"I can understand that," she said, nodding shakily. "I would feel the same way. So . . ."—she drew in a deep breath—"you can come over as often as you like."

He stared at her silently for a moment, then

pressed her hands tightly as though trying to give her some of his strength. "That wasn't exactly what I had in mind," he said, smiling cautiously. "Toby, I want us to get married."

Four

Toby sat frozen to the chair, her eyes widening when it seemed that he grew in size until he loomed over her stunned figure like a mysterious genie from a bottle. She couldn't force herself to form one single syllable, but had to sit listening to the word "married" clanging back and forth in her head as though Quasimodo himself were in there running amok in the belltower of Notre Dame.

"Ohhhhh," Toby moaned weakly. She closed her eyes and frantically gulped air into her lungs, then slid beneath the arm that suddenly extended across the chair. Mumbling inarticulate, breathless words, she made her way instinctively toward the kitchen.

"Where are you going?" Jake asked, two steps behind her. When she shook her head helplessly and kept walking, he said, "Toby, we need to talk about this. Toby—"

"Wait," she gasped, pulling open one cabinet

door after another, then slamming them shut in frustration. Finally, when she couldn't find even one stray peanut, she reached into the cookie jar and took a hurried bite of a chocolate cookie.

Oh, Oh, O-r-e-o. They keep your milk from getting lonely.

Milk, she thought frantically, as the lump of cookie in her throat refused to go down.

"Toby, what is wrong with you?"

Jake was standing directly behind her, and she could hear the frustration in his voice. She poured the milk faster, and after drinking half of it in one gulp she shrugged and whispered, "I had cookie caught in my throat." As though that explained everything.

She glanced out the window, then down at the glass in her hand, then at the bright yellow refrigerator. Anywhere but at the man standing a foot away from her. But when he moved to stand directly in front of her, she had to look at him.

She cleared her throat and glanced up at him hopefully. "You didn't really say what I thought you said . . . did you?"

He appeared to be torn between exasperation and amusement. "I said I want us to get married."

She inhaled a shaky breath. "That's what I was afraid of," she muttered. "Look, Mr. . . . Jake. I think you're taking this much too seriously." She tried to laugh, but failed completely. "This is the twentieth century. Nobody *has* to get married." Her voice grew more intense as she spoke. "Women are liberated, remember? We vote. We have careers. We even raise families all by ourselves. No one . . . *no one* expects a man to do the 'noble thing' anymore."

She looked up finally to find him watching her curiously. "You don't *have* to prove anything, Jake.

The secret is out. Men are fallible." She paused and smiled wistfully. "There are no more heroes, so you don't have to try to impress anyone with a sacrifice. This is simply not the age for grand gestures."

He reached out to tilt her chin up as though he were reminding her of his presence, as though he sensed she was talking of more than just their problem.

"Are you sure of that?" he asked quietly. "I can mention a half dozen real heroes without even thinking hard. For instance the priest on television last night who was almost singlehandedly taking on the drug dealers in his small neighborhood."

She moved away from him, then glanced back over her shoulder. "Don't you ever wonder what the so-called hero is getting out of it? Maybe it's the publicity. Maybe that particular man wants to move higher in the hierarchy of the church. I'd bet you'd be surprised how often there's a selfish motive behind that kind of thing."

She began to pace, unaware of the way he watched her thoughtfully, and the words came faster, her gesturing hands becoming more emphatic. "It always works that way. You think you've found something true blue, but underneath it's rotting. A government official is corrupt. A religious leader is embezzling church funds. Lots of doctors don't have practices, they have corporations. Some lawyers and policemen and judges are on the take. A few people in sports are using steroids to mess up their bodies—where have you gone, Joe Dimaggio?" she asked in a comically, helpless aside. "There are people blowing their brains out with drugs, then selling them to other people to support the habit—the drugs, that is, not the brains—because the brains aren't worth a nickel."

He was silent, staring at her in a way that made her increasingly uncomfortable. It was as though he could somehow see beyond her words to the inner workings of her mind. It made her feel more aware of him and in some strange way, vulnerable to that inquisitive stare of his.

"So skeptical," he murmured, shaking his head. "In the first place you're wrong about those things. In each case, you're taking a single example of bad and using it to condemn legions of people." He smiled and leaned against the counter. "And even if you were right, it has nothing to do with us. I'm not trying to make a grand gesture, and I'm definitely no hero. I'm just trying to do what's best."

"Best? How can it be right for two people who barely know each other to get married? I don't want to get married. And even if I did, what kind of marriage would it be?" She frowned suddenly and sat in a belligerent movement on the step stool beside the counter. "I can manage by myself. I don't need anyone to help me."

Jake moved to pull a chair from the small dinette set, then sat down in front of her, reaching out to capture her hands. "No one said you did," he said, his voice quiet, but urgent. "Toby, you said women raise children alone. And you're right," he added before she could interrupt. "I'm not questioning your strength or the strength of any woman for that matter." He smiled, silently encouraging her to relax. "In a lot of ways women are stronger than men. But you're asking your child to be strong along with you. Is that fair?"

"I don't know what you're talking about," she said defensively, keeping her eyes on the hands he still held.

"Look, Toby," he said gently. "I'll grant you that there are a lot of divorced women raising children . . . and doing a wonderful job of it. But you won't be divorced. You'll be single. And even if this is the twentieth century, some things haven't changed. Do you know what's going to happen the first time another kid asks our child where his father is? He can't say, 'My daddy went away,' or 'My parents are divorced.' He will have to say, 'My parents didn't get married.' Do you know what label they'll pin on him then?"

He paused, inhaling as he tightened his hold on her hands. "He'll be called a bastard, Toby. Maybe only once in his whole life, but it will happen. And do you have any idea what that will do to him?"

"No!" she gasped, jerking her head up to stare at him with wide, horrified eyes. "That doesn't happen anymore."

"Yes, it does."

He stood abruptly, releasing her hands, and moved to the small window above the sink. He stared silently out at the leaf-covered grounds that gently sloped down to a winding stream.

After a moment Toby glanced toward him, noticing his dark gray shirt and well-fitting black cord slacks. It was the first time she had seen him in casual dress, and in self-defense she shoved what was happening to the back of her mind to concentrate instead on the strength she could see beneath the soft fabric of his shirt.

He had seemed a large man to her on their first meeting, but she couldn't have guessed at the smooth, tight muscles his tailored jacket had concealed, the muscles she could see now in his taut back and shoulders.

Suddenly the vision of the beautiful bronze statue flashed unexplainably through her mind.

Where had she seen it? She visited all the local museums frequently, but she couldn't seem to recall which of them held the statue that kept popping into her mind. The lines, the purity of form suggested Greek sculpture, but which—

"Yes, it does," he repeated, and his quiet voice startled her, jerking her back to the present and all its problems.

"Especially here." He moved his shoulders as though trying to force his muscles to relax. "Even though Dallas is supposed to be one of the most cosmopolitan cities in the world, cosmopolitan is where we work, not where we live. It's still conservative." He paused, then continued in a low voice, "I had a friend, Toby. A good friend. She worked for me for two years before I really got to know her, but when I did, we hit it off right away. There was nothing romantic about it. We were, quite simply, friends. She . . . she had a baby. And she wasn't married. She was so damned proud of that baby." His voice was now tight with emotion. "At first neither of us heard the gossip, but gradually it became more bold." He glanced at her over his shoulder and said in a angry voice, "Before the baby was a year old, it got too much for her and she left. Not only her job but this part of the country."

He moved as though his thoughts made him uncomfortable. "The last time she called she seemed happy enough. But she's pretending to be a widow. She says she learned her lesson." He turned back to face her, seeming suddenly weary. "Okay, maybe, just maybe, it'll never happen. Can you take that chance? I can't," he muttered angrily. "I hated it when it happened to my goddaughter. I will not permit it to happen to my own child. Especially when it would be so easy to avoid."

Toby had been listening carefully to his slow, quiet words, had let him carry her along on his sad memory, and had begun to hurt for him. But this was too much, and she stared at him in astonishment.

"Easy?" she asked incredulously. "You're crazier than I am. Marrying someone you don't know is not easy. It is also not very smart." She lifted her hand in an emphatic gesture. "Seventy-eight point three percent of the marriages between people who have known each other less than two years fail," she said urgently, making up her facts on the spur of the moment. "Statistics don't lie. The whole thing is crazy!"

"It would be if we were expecting forever after," he said. "But we're not. All we have to do is get married. And live together . . . platonically," he added when he caught her wary look. "Then after the baby's born, we get a divorce."

She shook her head in wonder. "You make it sound so reasonable . . . so normal. When I know good and well it's not."

He sighed. "I think you're so busy fighting me and so uncomfortable around me that you aren't really thinking it through. I'm going to go now and let you think about it. Talk to Dr. Mathias and—what's your analyst's name?"

"Janine," she said vaguely, suddenly feeling swamped by the events of the past few days. "Janine White."

"Right," he said as he pushed away from the counter to walk into the living room. He turned and found her trailing helplessly behind. "Talk to Janine. See what both doctors think about it. I believe you'll discover that they don't think the idea is as outlandish as you do right now."

Sure, she thought in disbelief. *And maybe I'll*

find that my fairy godmother has turned me into a tall, willowy blonde too.

At the front door he stopped and turned around to face her, smiling slowly. "I know it seems like everything has been happening too fast, Toby. But you yourself said you were too busy coping to regret what's happened. That's what I'm doing. Trying to cope. Trying to do what's best for all of us."

He moved closer and reached out to cradle her neck, tilting her head with a gentle thumb on her chin. "Would it be so bad, being married to me?" he asked huskily. "I think we might turn out to be friends."

She stared at him silently, then her breathing became shallow when he leaned closer and brushed his lips across hers. Her eyelids fluttered down, and she felt the warmth he had brought to her mouth spread slowly through her limbs, leaving her bemused and lethargic.

She smiled in genuine surprise, opening her eyes slightly to find him watching her closely. "How *nice*," she breathed, then laughed softly. "Do it again," she whispered, unaware that she sounded like a child demanding the repeat of a treat.

He chuckled, the sound coming from deep in his throat as though she had taken him by surprise. Pulling her closer, he hugged her enthusiastically, and this time his kiss landed gently on the tip of her nose, then her forehead. It was nice, but not as nice as when he had kissed her lips.

"I have a feeling the next few months are going to be very interesting," he said, still chuckling quietly, then suddenly he was gone.

Toby stood before the door for quite a while, feeling confused and light-headed, but—oddly enough—very happy.

"What's really bothering you about all this?"

Toby slipped off her shoes, taking time to think over the question as she pulled her feet beneath her and leaned back in the large, modern chair facing Janine's desk. After a moment, she shifted her attention from her topaz pleated skirt to the woman who had begun to speak again.

"I don't think it's merely the unconventionality of marrying a stranger," Janine said in her firm analyst's voice. "You're not exactly a conventional person so it must be something else."

"What's really bothering me?" she said, giving a wry smile. "I'm pregnant, but to all intents and purposes, I've never made love. A man I don't know wants me to marry him and live with him who knows where until I have a baby that shouldn't be inside my body in the first place. A man with whom I feel extremely uncomfortable wants me to change my life so that I can feel uncomfortable all the time."

"And why do you feel uncomfortable around him?" came the carefully soothing question.

Toby shifted again, moving her hand to scratch the bottom of her foot. She always felt like the class problem child who had been sent to the principal's office when she visited Janine. The tall, thin brunette was very dignified, very conscious of being a successful professional woman. It seemed to Toby that Janine had taken it on herself to portray the perfect example of the New Woman. She always seemed to be trying so hard to prove there was no difference between women and men in the field of psychoanalysis. The only problem was she fought the battle so assiduously, she constantly pointed out that she was, in fact, different. If she could ever relax and simply be herself rather than always carrying the banner—Successful Professional Woman—it would have been far more convincing.

"Toby," Janine said, breaking into her thoughts. "You seem troubled about something." The calm brunette picked up a gold pencil and carefully pretended disinterest as she continued. "Exactly what happened during your meeting with this man?"

Toby watched her for a moment from beneath her eyelashes. The older woman's casual tone didn't fool her for a moment. She hid the mischief in her eyes and said hesitantly, "He . . . he—"

"Yes?" Janine prompted, leaning forward. "You know you can tell me anything."

"It all seemed so innocent in the beginning," Toby said softly, turning her head away. "But then . . ."

"Then?"

Janine was beginning to get impatient, and Toby almost sighed in relief as the woman's professional mask slipped away and the person beneath began to show.

"Then he started ripping his clothes off and chasing me around the apartment," Toby said enthusiastically, her hands moving to mime her words. "Well . . . well I can tell you, I was startled to say the least, but I held my own, Janine. I didn't give in. I didn't even get nervous until he caught me—"

"Toby," Janine said, sighing in quiet resignation.

"—in the bathroom and pulled out a lo-o-ong silk whip. It was red and—"

"*Toby.*"

"—and it matched his red leather bikini underwear and his red leather sweat socks." She opened her eyes wide. "And you wouldn't believe what he wanted me to do. He wanted me to—"

"Toby!"

Toby leaned forward and smiled ingenuously, then when she saw the exasperated amusement in the other woman's face, they both began to laugh.

"Okay, smart aleck," Janine said ruefully. "You've spent enough time making fun of me. Now do you want to tell me why you feel uncomfortable around this man? You've always felt uneasy around men so I assume this is something entirely different."

Toby thought about that for a moment, then said slowly, "Yes, it is. And I think that's what worries me. Before all I had to be concerned about was a curly stomach and sweaty hands. With him, something else happens. I feel things I've never felt before. Things happen to my body when I'm around him. They make me . . . oh, I don't know. I just don't know how to handle it."

She shrugged in frustration, resting her elbow on the arm of the chair to prop her chin in her palm. "Everything was going along fine. I was able to live with the way I am. I had accepted the way I feel around men, and I knew what to expect. Then suddenly this happens, and I have to learn to cope all over again."

Janine was thoughtfully silent for a moment, then she said slowly, "Is it possible that what you feel for this man is physical attraction?"

"No!" Toby gasped without thinking, then clenching her fists, she forced herself to calm down. "I've never been physically attracted to a man before," she whispered. "Why should it be any different now?"

"That's a heavy question. Why is any person attracted to another? It's not simply their appearance that does it. It's something extra. Maybe chemical. Maybe mental. Who knows?"

"I certainly don't," Toby muttered under her breath. "Why is it so important anyway?"

Janine swung her chair to the side and leaned back. "It's important because I think you are going to decide that marrying him is the right thing for you. Just as you decided that abortion was the wrong thing for you. And if you do you'll need to work out your feelings for him or you won't last until the baby's born. I don't want the relationship to throw you any traumatic curves."

"There is no relationship," she said emphatically, then warily, "What kind of curves?"

Janine chuckled. "You'll be living in the same house with this man. Suppose he tries to kiss you?"

"Well, actually . . . he did that already," Toby mumbled, shifting in her chair. Then she glanced up to see Janine staring at her with raised eyebrows.

"Oh? And how did you feel about that?"

She eagerly inclined her body toward Janine. "It was the strangest thing, Janine. I didn't feel desire . . . I think that would have made me sick to my stomach. It caused the weirdest tingling all the way down to my bones and I felt warm all over . . . like taking a hot bath from the inside out."

Janine stared at her strangely for a moment, then picked up the gold pencil again and said casually, "But you believe that experiencing desire would make you feel sick?"

"I know it would," Toby said ruefully. "I've thought about it before and just thinking about it made me sick, but this was different." Her eyes were open wide in surprise. "Why, it was really . . . nice."

Janine stared down at the pencil in her hands for a moment, then sighed. "Well, if it made you feel warm and nice, then of course it couldn't be desire, could it? So I suppose there's really nothing to worry about if you decide to marry him."

"I don't know about that," she muttered. "The kissing was nice, but talking to him is a whole different thing. It makes me uncomfortable. And sometimes he watches me. Very quietly and very intently. It's murder not knowing what is going through his mind."

"I believe that's something you'll get used to once you've been around him awhile." Janine glanced at her watch and Toby knew her hour was almost up. "Everyone has to make adjustments. Does he scare you?"

"I don't think so. . . . well, maybe sometimes," Toby amended, habitually honest. "But most of the time I'm just confused."

"Well, since you won't really be married, I don't imagine there will be any problems you can't handle." When Janine stood up, Toby uncurled and slipped into her shoes, then they walked together to the door. "It won't be that much of a change in your life," Janine continued with an odd little smile. "Like he said, it's not forever. You'll simply be rooming with him for a while."

No big thing, Toby. And if you happen to stumble across him reading the newspaper in his underwear, just pretend you got him with green stamps.

She glanced at Janine warily. "So you think I should do it?"

"That's up to you, Toby. You'll have to decide what *you* think you should do."

Toby spotted the empty park bench and struggled to hold on to her popcorn, purse, and shopping bag at the same time. The popcorn was just about to go when she reached the bench at last and sat down.

Relaxing with a sigh, she threw a handful of popcorn in the direction of a small oak tree. Very few birds were in sight, but she knew from experience they would spot the popcorn within seconds after it hit the ground.

She watched the pigeons feeding for a few moments, then rested against the bench. She recalled the way Janine had smiled when she had said that there wouldn't be that much of a change in her life. Toby frowned suddenly. It was as though her analyst knew something that Toby didn't.

Which is a distinct possibility, Toby thought wryly. Because right at the moment she felt she knew nothing at all. She had turned the problem over and over in her mind and seemed no closer to the answer now than she had been before.

Dr. Mathias, too, had been very sympathetic, very kind, when Toby had called her, but had given her no pat answers. She also said it was up to Toby to decide. Her parting sentence had been, "I'm sure you'll do the right thing, Toby."

I'm glad she knows that, Toby thought, throwing another handful of popcorn in a short, frustrated movement. Because she wasn't all that sure she would do the right thing. She didn't even know what the right thing was.

Was "right" ever all that certain? Why did they make it seem as though someone handed you a guidebook that had all the "right things" listed in the back? How could they all—Janine, Dr. Mathias, and Jake—be so sure there was a right way? Because so often the right of the present turned out to be the wrong of the future.

She shook her head. Where did they come by their assurance? They all seemed so positive—about everything. Toby had never in her life been that positive—about anything. She couldn't remember ever having made a major decision. She had always floated helplessly along on currents that she had no control over, trying to keep from tipping the boat, struggling to bail the water out faster than it poured in.

But now somehow that seemed wrong. She had been told—and she felt herself—that she should be taking charge of her life, and the thought overwhelmed her. It was like asking a third-grade room monitor to run the country.

Toby jerked her head up suddenly as she felt the bench move. She glanced at the thin man beside her, then smiled when she recognized her old friend, Lyell the Philosopher. At least that was his title here at the small park that Toby frequented. She had met Lyell three years earlier and had been immediately fascinated by his disregard for conventions and his irreverent comments on anything that represented the establishment.

"The birds are hungry this morning," he said gruffly, leaning back so the sun caught and sparkled in his magnificent white mane of hair. "Do you think if we keep feeding them they might one day turn up their noses at popcorn and bread crumbs and demand Black Forest torte?"

Toby giggled. "They would have to wear teeny, tiny three-piece suits and Italian leather shoes."

"No, no," he said emphatically. "Italian leather is 'out' at the moment. We mustn't have passé pigeons."

Toby sobered suddenly as her problem refused to

stay hidden even during a leisurely and amusing talk. She turned distracted eyes to the man beside her. "Lyell, I suppose you must have made a lot of decisions in your life. How do you know when you're doing the 'right thing'?"

"That's a tough one, Toby," he said, ruefully rubbing his cheek. "And since I've been a bum for a good many years now, I may not be the best one to advise you."

Toby let her gaze drift over the man beside her. He was meticulously dressed, his tie tied just so, his suit pressed and neat. But when she looked closer, she saw the worn fabric, the almost invisible mending that had been done.

"Are you a bum?" she asked, turning toward him, her eyes intrigued.

"The truth of that is a matter that has been much debated among my colleagues with no satisfactory conclusion being reached, but to all intents and purposes—yes, I am," he said sounding very satisfied. "I spent a lot of years trying to do the 'right thing,' my dear, then it suddenly occurred to me that my idea of right was in no way related to the general consensus."

He paused and inhaled deeply, savoring the crisp fall air as though it were a fine wine. "And since there was no one to be hurt by my living up to my own definition of right, I did just that. I now feel no obligation to top my neighbor, only to love him. And when I teach, I only teach people who are hungry to learn." He indicated the park around him. "This is my classroom now."

"You were a teacher?"

"I was professor of philosophy at a very grand university," he said, smiling. "And I stood before a room full of very grand young people. I don't say taught because very few of them listened to what I was so earnestly saying. I soon determined that the ones who wanted to learn would learn without me. The others were there to buy a document to hang on their walls."

Toby threw out the last of her popcorn, thoughtfully silent for a moment, then she said slowly, "You said there was no one to influence your decision to be a . . . a . . ."

"A bum?"

"A gentleman of leisure," she amended with a laugh. "What if there had been? Suppose you had had . . . say—a child? One that was too young to voice an opinion?"

"Ah, now we're speaking of an entirely different proposition," he said, and Toby could see him warming to the subject. "Being responsible for another human being is a wondrous, terrifying thing. You can never make a decision based on your wants, your needs, without considering how it will affect the other person involved." He smoothed his elegant mustache with one finger, and she could almost see him standing behind the podium at his Ivy League university.

"I've found, Toby, that you can never be truly happy if you hurt other people in the process. It's marvelous, of course, if you can make a decision that is best not only for the other person but also for you. But I'm afraid it rarely works that way. Usually you just grit your teeth and do your duty."

Duty? Yes, she decided with a small nod. She had a duty to her child. He couldn't speak for himself. It was up to her to do the right thing. Not the right thing for Toby Baxter, but the right thing for a baby that didn't ask to be conceived. It had nothing to do with the strange activities of its parents. So Toby had to do what was best for it.

Again she heard Jake's question. *Can you take*

that chance? And suddenly she knew she couldn't. The best as far as Toby could see was to give her child a name. And to allow its father the privilege of being in on its birth. So many men wouldn't have cared. This man did, and she owed it to her baby to let him get as close as he wanted to.

So the decision was made. And right or wrong she would stick by it. She glanced down at her watch. There was no need in putting it off.

Crumpling her empty popcorn bag, she stood up and tossed it into a nearby trash container, then, inhaling deeply, she smiled down at Lyell.

"Thank you, Lyell. You've done what my analyst couldn't. You gave a clear path to follow. I can adjust to the change."

She had already picked up her purse and shopping bag and begun to walk away before Lyell began to recover from her sudden departure.

"Wait, Toby," he shouted after her. "What are you going to change?"

"My life," she called back with unfamiliar determination, then smiled and kept walking.

Five

Toby walked around her little white M. G. and moved up the walk to the front door. She stood for a moment on the doorstep of Jake's home, finishing her peanuts as she looked around her. The house was in an older, quieter part of Dallas. The part that was always spoken of in a tone of voice tinged with a little hushed awe.

However not by Toby. Her parents had lived in this same section of Dallas during the years that Toby was growing up, and it was familiar to her. No children played on the manicured lawns or raced down the sidewalks. There were no teenagers working on cars while Boy George serenaded them at a deafening level. All was quiet and dignified—on the surface. But Toby knew what went on—and what did not go on—inside these distinguished houses, and the memory of loneliness brought on an uncontrollable shiver.

She carefully steadied her breathing until the

tightness in her stomach disappeared, then rang the doorbell. Almost immediately the door was opened by a pleasant looking woman in her early sixties or late fifties.

"Is Mr. Hammond in?" Toby asked shyly.

"Yes, miss," she said, then the woman Toby assumed was Jake's housekeeper gave her an encouraging smile. "Who should I say is calling?"

"Me—that is—Toby," she stuttered, then closed her eyes and said, "Toby Baxter."

Mr. Hammond's housekeeper stated to the press that the mad woman appeared on their doorstep late in the afternoon and began to drool crazily all over the handmade welcome mat.

When Toby looked up the woman was staring at her expectantly, indicating a door off the entry hall. Following quickly, Toby almost moaned in frustration when she tripped over a rug.

She could see the older woman hiding a smile as she left the room. After a moment she shrugged in resignation and began to examine the small, sunny room.

Outside she had seen similarities to her own childhood home, but in here no such similarities could be found. There was life and vitality here that had been missing in Toby's home. She moved to the small fireplace and studied the pictures on the mantle. The one that held her attention was of a younger Jake and two women, both older than he. She searched the feminine faces for a family resemblance and at first found none, but as soon as she leaned closer she saw what she was looking for. There was a strength—mellowed, but present nonetheless in both women—about the chin and eyes.

"Toby?"

The soft question was spoken from directly

behind her, and she whirled around to find Jake standing in the doorway, watching her with a puzzled look in his eyes.

"You've got a lovely home," she said quietly, clasping her hands together.

He nodded, still staring, then shook his head and smiled. "Come into the study. We only use this room when the minister comes to call."

"It's nice."

He took her elbow and led her down the hall to a large room. The wall facing the back yard was made entirely of glass, allowing the wild tangle of the seemingly natural garden to invade the room. On her left she saw a fire in the large brick fireplace, and when she smelled the burning wood it seemed as though they were beside a campfire in the open woods. The colors of the room were a warm blend of the colors of fall, and she wondered with a small smile if he changed the decor to suit the seasons.

Jake led her to a loveseat beside the fire, then after they were seated waited expectantly for a moment. When the uneasy silence continued, he said wryly, "It's not that I'm not glad to see you, but why are you here, Toby? I thought I was supposed to come to your apartment later tonight."

"Well," she said in a gusty sigh. "I made up my mind and I decided there was no reason to wait. . . . So here I am."

His face changed suddenly, and the tension brought back the expressionless mask she had seen before in his office. "You've made your decision?" He shifted his position to stare into the fire, leaning his forearms on his thighs. The muscles in his arms and shoulders were tight and stiff, matching his voice as he asked, "And what have you decided?"

"Was there ever any real choice?" she asked quietly, shrugging. "You were right. I can't take a chance on harming the child. He can't speak for himself yet, so I have to speak for him. And I think he would like to have his father's name on his birth certificate."

Jake didn't say anything, but his head slumped forward. He exhaled slowly as though he had been holding his breath, and the tight muscles seemed to relax one by one. Then he turned to face her, and the unbelievable joy on his face made her catch her breath. She felt a strange emotion race through her. It was intense satisfaction. Satisfaction that she could have spoken the words to give him such pleasure.

"Toby," he whispered hoarsely, moving closer to take her hands and squeeze them tightly. "That's . . . that's fine. Just fine. I'm . . . I'm glad you didn't wait." He drew in a breath, then exhaled in shaky laugh. "We have a lot to do. Where would you like to get married?" Before she could answer he went on, standing to pace a few steps away. "We can get our blood tests tomorrow. . . . And I think if we hustle we could get married on Saturday." He paused and seemed to be speaking to himself more than to Toby. "My church has a beautiful little chapel that would be perfect. I hope it isn't already reserved for Saturday."

"But that's only three days from now!" she gasped, jumping to her feet.

"Right, three days," he said, giving her a distracted glance. "But it will go quickly. We have to move your things here."

"*Wait*," she said desperately. "Jake, it's happening too fast. Why are we going to move my things here, and why are we going to reserve a chapel? I thought we would just go to a justice of the peace for a brief ceremony." She sighed. "Should it be a religious service?"

"Are you an atheist?" he said looking at her curiously.

"No-o-o. I mean, of course not," she said, shaking her head in confusion. "That's just the point. Should we ask God's blessing for a marriage that we plan to dissolve after the baby's born?"

"Well, He would know that, wouldn't He?" he asked, not even trying to hide his amused smile. "And if everything weren't completely on the up and up, I'm sure He wouldn't bless it no matter where we were married. But don't you want His blessing on our mutual parenthood?"

"I didn't think of that," she said weakly. "Yes, of course, that makes sense. But what about my moving in here? I . . . I didn't really think about it, but I guess I assumed we would be staying at my apartment. It's familiar to me, you see."

"Yes, I do see." His confident, self-assured voice calmed her a little. "But I still think it would be better if we stayed here. You'll need help when you come home from the hospital. Mrs. Pratt will be here to give you that help."

"Oh." Toby rubbed her chin with the palm of her hand as she thought about that. Everything he said was reasonable and made sense, so why did she get the feeling that things were moving too fast? That in some way she was being railroaded into doing things she should think over more carefully?

"Yes . . . okay. . . . I guess you're right," she said vaguely, then looked up sharply when he stepped closer to give her a quick hug.

"Toby," he said sternly as she watched him in wary fascination. "I thought we decided it wasn't unusual for the father of a child to touch the mother of that same child."

"Unusual? No-o-o. I guess it's not unusual. It's just that I'm not used to . . . this kind of thing. Will there be a lot of it . . . afterward?" She glanced at him suspiciously. "I thought it was supposed to be platonic."

He smiled and said softly, "Does platonic mean cold? Lots of friends hug and kiss, but there's nothing sexual about it."

She couldn't keep her muscles from contracting when he said the word "sexual." Avoiding his eyes, she moistened her lips nervously. "I've never had a kissing, hugging friend," she said, her voice growing thoughtful. "Nevertheless, I suppose I'll get used to it."

She looked up with a rueful smile. "I guess it's about time I tackled the touching thing. I suppose it must be because my parents weren't demonstrative people. I didn't really notice how odd it was until about a year ago."

She moved away and resumed her seat on the couch, pulling her feet up beside her after slipping off her shoes. When she saw the questions in his eyes, she continued.

"Lynda and I were taking some children on a picnic—we both work with handicapped kids in a local hospital on the weekend—and she saw one of them climbing a tree and wanted to get my attention. She put her hand on my shoulder, and I turned around to look at her." She grimaced. "I have no idea what my face looked like, but suddenly she jerked her hand away. It made me feel very strange. I felt I had hurt her feelings, but I didn't know what to do about it."

She looked up at him suddenly and nodded emphatically. "Yes, I think I would very much like to stop feeling like that. It may turn out to be very nice having a touching friend."

He didn't speak for a moment. He stared straight ahead, then in a strange distracted voice, he said, "Yes. Yes, it just might at that."

Jake pulled his hands out from under his head and raised himself to rest against the headboard. The trousers of his brown silk pajamas slid lower on his lean, hard hips, and in the dim lighting the flesh of his bare chest looked unusually dark against the cream pillow cases.

Lighting a cigarette, he stared at the pattern of dark and light on the ceiling, wondering what Toby was doing now. He should have insisted that they spend this last evening together. She was still wary about marrying him, and he didn't want the doubts to get out of hand. If he had been able to think of a good reason to invade the get-together she had planned with her friends tonight, he would be there now even though he knew he didn't have the right to intrude. Not yet anyway.

The past two days had flown by. The blood tests. The marriage license. Moving her clothing and personal things to his house.

He laughed now, recalling the look on her face when she had seen his bedroom on her tour of the house. Her eyes had widened at the size of it, then the strangest look had come over her face, making him wonder for a moment if she did remember the night they had spent together.

He shook his head, sending the vision flying, then reached for the telephone, and before he could drag up all the very good reasons not to, he punched out her number. Annoyance and concern mingled on his face by the time the phone was picked up on the fifth ring and he heard her voice.

"Toby," he began, then heard the noise in the background. "Toby, what's going on?"

"Jake," she said, her voice loud as though she couldn't hear herself above the noise. "Lynda and the gang from the hospital decided to throw me a bachelor party, and as you can hear it's getting a little noisy. Lynda . . ." Her voice faded as though she were turning away from the phone. "Lynda, tell him not to take off anything else. Oh, dear. I don't think she heard me."

"Toby! What in hell's happening? Who's there?"

"Someone sent one of those singing telegrams. Actually it's a singing, dancing telegram, but I don't think anyone has noticed that he's singing." Her voice faded again as she repeated, "Lynda, tell him . . ." Then there was a long pause. "Oh, *my*," she said finally in quiet astonishment.

"Toby Baxter," he said, gritting his teeth in exasperation. "If you don't tell me this minute what's going on, I'm coming over."

"Oh, that's not necessary, Jake," she said quickly.

"*Toby*," he said in quiet, deadly frustration.

"Really, Jake. It's all right. It doesn't scare me. I guess because of all the people here." He could hear someone close to her speak, then she said, "I've got to go, Jake. I'm fine. . . . I promise." Then all was silent as she broke the connection.

He didn't stop to think over what he was doing as he stood abruptly and began to pull on his clothes. Ten minutes later he was in his car and pushing it past the speed limit in the direction of her apartment.

As he drove, he kept puzzling over what she had said. Why on earth should it scare her? And what was it about Toby that made him think she was fragile? That the wrong move or the wrong word would crush her?

Dr. Mathias had said there was something in her past that she couldn't speak of because it was privileged information. What? It was driving him crazy. Toby was an extremely attractive woman— an extremely appealing woman. Why had she been a virgin until the night she spent with him? She seemed unusually shy and ignorant of the mating games men and women played. Women her age usually had the art of casual flirtation down pat. But not Toby.

Dr. Mathias had said no one could be around Toby for long without being captivated, and now Jake's lips moved in a self-mocking smile as he admitted the truth of her statement. Toby seemed to be in his thoughts constantly.

He pulled into the parking lot of her apartment building and stepped from the car, his movements quick and fluid. Now that he had had time to calm down, he wondered why he was here at all. Toby had said she didn't need his help, and he admitted ruefully that he couldn't very well go in and throw everyone out.

He stood for a moment, then shrugged impatiently and rang the bell. When she opened the door enough to see him standing in the hall, he looked beyond her into the apartment and frowned when he saw that the room behind her was empty.

"What happened to the party?" he said as he walked in and began to survey the cluttered room.

Toby laughed and leaned down to pick up scattered wrappings and ribbon. "They decided to move it to Lynda's apartment. I pleaded a headache." She grinned. "It works every time."

Stooping to pick up a box from the floor, he gently lifted a frothy piece of apricot lace from the box.

It seemed to consist entirely of two small rectangles held together by impossibly small satin ribbons. He stared at it a moment, intrigued, then, raising one eyebrow in amusement, threw Toby a questioning glance.

She grabbed it from him hastily, then laughed again softly, this time with a nervous catch in her throat. "My friends have some pretty strange ideas about what one should wear to bed."

He smiled a slow, unconsciously sensual smile. "Strange? I wouldn't exactly describe it like that."

"No?" She looked at him curiously, tilting her head slightly, then murmured, "How very odd." She moved hesitantly to the center of the room with the scraps of lace clutched to her breasts. "Jake, why are you here? It's not that I'm not glad to see you," she said quickly as though she were afraid of hurting his feelings. "It's just that . . . well, I'll see you first thing in the morning. Was there something you needed before then?"

Something he needed, he thought, his smile becoming strained as he stared at the lace pressed to her breasts. A loaded question if he'd ever heard one. "I just wanted to make sure you're all right. That you're not getting cold feet." He glanced around, grimacing. "Maybe it's a good thing I came by. You look like you could use some help."

"Oh, don't worry about that," she said, making a face at the clutter. "I've got a few things still in the closet to pack, then I'm through with that. As for the mess, my cleaning woman said she would come by tomorrow to take care of this. Then she'll stop by twice a month to air things out and dust."

He nodded slowly. She was already thinking about the time when she could come back to this place. He didn't think he liked being considered a temporary inconvenience. Moving to the sofa, he watched silently as she gathered up her gifts. He hated to admit how much he enjoyed watching Toby. He hadn't known a small woman could move so beautifully.

She didn't speak when she left the room with her arms full, but glanced at him with a small smile that caused his muscles to tighten inexplicably. He sat bemused for a moment, then irritated at the strange emotions that were attacking him, he jerkily picked up the red and gold leather-bound album that lay on a low shelf next to him.

He thumbed through it distractedly for a moment, then began to take in the photos it contained. On the first few pages were pictures of an attractive couple. By their clothes he assumed the photographs were taken in the late forties. He glanced over the wedding pictures, then pictures of the same couple in casual dress standing in front of the fountain of Trevi and the Spanish steps in Rome.

There were pages and pages of photographs of the two people before he came across one page containing pictures of them holding a smiling round-faced baby. He turned to the next page hoping for more photos of the child he knew to be Toby, but except for one of a ten-year-old Toby in formal riding dress next to a beautiful horse and a picture of her graduating from high school, there were no more. There were pictures of another child, a boy, but no caption to indicate who he was.

He glanced up as Toby reentered the room. "Where are the other pictures?"

"Other pictures?"

"The ones of you when you were growing up. I want to see what our child will look like."

She laughed uneasily. "If he's lucky it won't be like me. I was a horrid-looking baby. In fact that's how I got my name according to Father. He said I looked like a Toby jug. You know those pitchers that look like fat men with cocked hats?"

He studied her until she shifted uncomfortably. "I've seen them, and you don't look like them in the least."

"I did when I was a baby," she assured him, moving closer.

"I saw only three pictures of you when you were a baby, and that wasn't enough to tell. Don't you have one of you lying on a bearskin rug?"

"'Fraid not," she said, shrugging. "Those are the only ones I have. I don't think my parents were into taking pictures."

Not of you anyway, he thought, feeling an unreasonable anger toward her parents. The album was full of pictures of the two of them. But Toby had been the subject of only half a dozen. He glanced down quickly at the album before she could read the antagonism in his face.

"And who's this?"

"Who? I haven't looked at that in so long, I probably won't recognize some of the people."

She leaned across the back of the couch to look over his shoulder. The photo he had picked at random was of a handsome man in army uniform. Decorations were spread ostentatiously across his chest. He was an impressive looking figure, but not austere. There was a smile in his eyes, and one could tell his lips were ready to smile at any moment. His cap was tilted slightly, giving him the look of a lovable, devil-may-care rogue.

When Toby remained silent, he glanced at her curiously to find her staring at the photo.

"That's Uncle Paul," she whispered, her voice strangely hoarse.

"He was your father's brother or your mother's?"

She shook her head and turned away. "He was neither. He was . . ." She drew in a deep breath "It was an . . . affectionate title."

He could feel the tension in her and watched her closely. She was strangely pale. She turned suddenly and mumbled, "Excuse me," then rushed out of the room.

"Toby—" he began, but she didn't stop.

He sat still for a minute, glancing back at the album in confusion, searching for a clue to her actions. There were more pictures of the man she called Uncle Paul than there were of Toby. Pictures of him tall and tanned in tennis shorts and V-neck sweater. Pictures that showed his laughing face and well-built figure in ski clothes against a backdrop of crisp, white snow.

There was nothing there to show why Toby had acted so strangely, and when she didn't return in a few minutes, Jake became uneasy with the silence of the apartment. Standing quickly, he moved across the room and went through the door she had taken.

It was her bedroom. A lamp was switched on beside the small bed that looked somehow lonely in the large room—which was empty.

"Toby?" he said softly, moving to the bathroom, but it too was empty.

He stood puzzled for a moment, wondering what in hell was going on, then he heard movement behind the other door that he had assumed was a closet. Moving quickly, he opened it and found he was right. It was a closet. And sitting on the floor in the middle of a scattering of shoes was Toby.

She sat with her arms wrapped around her knees, rubbing her chin with the toe of a green suede shoe. After a moment, she looked up at him, then back at the wall.

He stared down at her for a moment, then stepped inside and closed the door softly behind him, lowering himself to sit beside her, about a foot away. When his eyes had adjusted to the dark, he slowly reached out and picked up her hand.

"Do you want to tell me about your Uncle Paul?"

"No."

Her voice was soft and feminine, but totally uncompromising.

"Do you want to tell me why you're sitting in a closet?" he asked, carefully keeping the concern out of his voice.

She laughed, and her voice held relief and a very real amusement. "It's a habit, I guess." She paused, turning her head to look at him, and added thoughtfully, "Janine would probably say it's an attempt to return to the security of the womb."

"Do you think so?"

"Not really. My mother and I were never that close." When she spoke again her voice held a touch of mischief. "I can just imagine the look on her face if I tried to return to the womb. After she got over the shock she would probably very calmly have me committed and say she always knew I was a little strange."

He laughed, then they fell into a comfortable silence. After a few moments he raised his arm and let it come to rest around her shoulders. She held herself stiff at first, then he could feel her relax, and she sighed and moved closer. "You were right. It is nice having a touching friend."

"I hope you'll always think so," he murmured, brushing the hair from her forehead. "Another thing about friends, Toby, is that they can tell each other anything. Part of accepting a friend is allowing them into your thoughts and feelings."

"Lynda doesn't feel that way," she said, sounding faintly defensive. "At least she's never said so."

"But she's not a hugging, kissing friend is she?"

"No. You're right." She paused, inhaling slowly. When she spoke again her voice was stiff and cold in a way he hadn't heard before. "Uncle Paul was my parents' best friend. After Tommy died he was their only real friend."

"Tommy?"

"My younger brother," she said in a pained whisper. "You probably saw his pictures in the album. My parents thought the world began the day Tommy was born . . . and I guess for us it did. He was so full of life, and he carried that life into every corner of our world. I guess that's one of the reasons I decided to work at the children's hospital as well as at the day care center during the week. I thought I might find a little of what Tommy gave me with those other children. After a while it wasn't for Tommy anymore, it was for them. They all give love so freely to anyone who wants it." She was silent for a long time, remembering. "Then when Tommy was six, he died in one of those crazy playground accidents that happen to children all the time with less drastic results. He fell from a swing and hit his head."

She shifted her position as if the subject was still difficult to talk about. "My parents had never been openly affectionate, but after Tommy died they withdrew even more. It took me quite a while to realize that they were both afraid . . . afraid to love too much . . . afraid they might be hurt again. The only person they really opened up to after Tommy's death was Uncle Paul. He was a hero of the Korean War. The perfect man in their eyes. Maybe they thought that since he had made it through a war he was safe to love."

Silence fell again as he turned her words over in his mind. "Were you jealous of him?" he asked softly. "Did you feel he was taking something that was yours?"

She tensed suddenly. "Maybe," she said in a small, strained voice. "Maybe I was without knowing it."

She was still holding something back. He knew it as surely as if she had given him the key to her mind. Jealousy wasn't the clue to what Toby was all about. From the photos he had seen of her parents, he couldn't see any warmth in the people who had given her life. He had felt empty as he had looked at them. But the other man—the man called Paul—had a friendly, smiling face and laughing eyes. He would have to make an impression on someone as lonely as the child Jake had seen in those few photographs of Toby. Paul had been someone who laughed with her and hugged her, instead of scolding her and ignoring her.

"Were you close to Paul?" He felt her jerky nod. "Maybe you were jealous of the hold your parents had on him. Maybe you wanted him to spend all his time with you."

"Yes," she whispered tightly, and he heard a new element in her soft voice. If he hadn't known better, he would have said it was venom—even hatred.

"I was," she continued. "He loved me. Openly and warmly. They didn't." Her voice became hoarse. "Is it any wonder that I wanted to be around him all the time?"

"And then he died?"

"Yes." She laughed, and the sound made his hair stand on end. "Yes, the hero died," she ground out harshly. "But not before he had killed all the heroes."

She began to tremble violently, and his arms

tightened around her. For a long time they stayed that way as he murmured soothing, unintelligible words in her ear and stroked her hair with a hand that trembled.

He mentally berated himself for stumbling unawares into what was obviously a hurtful area for her. He was afraid he had pushed her too far. There was something here that he desperately wanted the answer to, but now was not the time. It was something that would have to happen gradually.

When he felt the tremors in her body cease, he tilted her chin and stared down at her. Her face was solemn in the light that filtered in around the door. Smiling slowly, he gave her a reassuring squeeze and said softly, "Do you have any coffee in here?"

For a moment she looked stunned, then she laughed in delight. As his eyes widened in pleased astonishment, she gave him a fleeting kiss of gratitude.

Before he could stop himself, his hand went to the back of her neck to hold the kiss, and he felt the pleasure rush through his body in a flood of warmth.

If he had felt any hesitation in her at all, he would have backed off immediately, but he felt none. There was nothing to stop him from deepening the kiss. Nothing to keep him from tasting her, from rediscovering the texture of her lips the way that so often he had relived the experience from the night they had spent together.

For long moments she remained perfectly still, then miraculously, like a butterfly unfolding its wings, her lips moved beneath his, and he had to clamp down on the urge to shout in triumph. He couldn't however, prevent a low moan of pleasure from escaping him as he pulled her across his legs and settled her in his lap.

"Jake—" she whispered hoarsely as he moved his mouth to the soft, fragrant skin of her neck.

"Um?"

She swallowed to begin to speak again, and he felt the muscles of her throat ripple under his lips. "Jake, how do you do that?" she murmured slowly.

"Do what?" His hand had somehow slipped to her hips and was applying a subtle downward pressure as the muscles of his thighs tightened in an uncontrollable upward movement. His mind was flooded with memories of the way she had looked that night, the way she had felt. He wanted that again. He *had* to have that again.

"Make that crazy tingle?" she whispered. "When I was a child—" She stopped speaking and caught her breath when his lips slid lower to follow the line of her delicate collarbone. "When I was a child, my friends and I used to get a kick out of touching our tongues to flashlight batteries. This is the same thing. Only . . . only more and deeper."

Her hand moved on his neck, molding the tendons as though she were fascinated by the touch of him beneath her fingers. He could feel the aching hardness of his arousal pressing into her soft buttocks, and he knew he would have to stop now or take a chance on losing all control. He desperately wanted to lower her to the floor of the closet and have her lying beneath him, soft and supple and sensuous the way she had been that night. He wanted to know again, now, the urgency that had been in her then. He wanted . . .

Swallowing a groan, he removed her hand from his neck and held it tightly in his. "I think we'd better get that coffee now," he said brusquely. He realized at once that his voice held a harshness he hadn't intended, and he tried to soften it by brushing a kiss across her forehead.

"The coffee?" she asked in a faint, bewildered whisper, then she gave a small, rueful laugh. "Oh, dear, I'd forgotten. I'm afraid I'm not a very good hostess, but believe it or not, I'm not used to entertaining in the closet."

She gave his hand a quick—almost affectionate—squeeze and moved, bracing herself on his shoulder to stand.

"Believe it or not," he echoed huskily, "I'm not used to being entertained in a closet. But I can see now that it has definite potential. The possibilities boggle the mind."

She laughed gaily, and as he stood to follow her out of the dark, incredibly sweet hidey-hole, he wondered about the exploding joy her voluntary kiss had brought. About his inability to remain objective when he held her close to him. There was no doubt about it. He was getting involved with Toby. Not as the mother of his child, not as a young woman who needed help, but as a beautiful, desirable woman.

He had come charging over here tonight not to make sure she hadn't changed her mind, but because he didn't like the idea of her being with a man. Any man, even one who was hired to deliver best wishes.

And as if that were not enough, he mused with a rough smile as he walked behind her to the kitchen, there was another idea that kept haunting him. There had to be some reason that Toby was carrying his child when he had thought it an impossibility. Surely there had to be some greater plan of destiny working here. Because if she and only she had conceived a child by him, why not another . . . and another? He could not force away the belief that in some way their lives were meant to be entwined.

Six

Toby stood in the middle of the large reception hall and let the music and the sound of laughter and conversation flow around her stunned figure. She smiled continuously, trying to pretend she wasn't mentally and physically exhausted.

She had done it. She had really, actually, honest-to-gosh done it. She cut her eyes to the side to sneak a glimpse of the man beside her, then looked away hurriedly, running her hands nervously down the slim skirt of the bisque-colored dress that, combined with a frivolous little veiled hat, made up her wedding ensemble.

Oh, yes, she thought with a shaky sigh, she had actually married a man she knew almost nothing about.

Then as she felt his supporting hand come about her waist, as she felt the warmth of it penetrate her flesh, she realized she was wrong. She knew what she needed to know about Jake. She knew he was kind and concerned. She knew that bringing a new life into the world really mattered to him and that he would be a wonderful father. For a temporary roommate that was a lot to know.

In fact, for anyone that was a lot. She smiled sadly as she thought of the telegram she had sent to her parents, informing them of her marriage, and the one she had received from them in return this morning. It had been short and not very sweet, but Toby hadn't really expected more. They had very calmly wished her well and informed her that she could expect a sizable check in the mail.

Their offhand attitude would probably seem strange to anyone else, but Toby knew them and had gradually come to accept them as they were. She was also honest enough with herself to acknowledge that their presence at her wedding would have made the occasion even more difficult for her.

So much of the day was blurred as she thought of it now, but certain incidents stood out vividly, as though they had been saved to flash through her mind with the intense clarity of three-dimensional slides.

The sun streaming through a wall of stained glass windows. The smell of the gardenias she carried. The unexpected tears that had formed in her eyes when she had seen the children from the day care center and the hospital—her children—looking unnaturally angelic as they watched her walk down the aisle. The very real warmth in the minister's voice. Her audible gasp when she glanced down at the ring Jake was slipping on her finger. The feel of Jake's lips on hers, the reassuring clasp of his hand.

She looked down at her ring again now, and the size and beauty of it took her breath away.

"Do you like it?"

Glancing up quickly, she found Jake watching her expectantly. After an almost imperceptible pause, he asked again, "Do you like the ring, Toby?"

"How could I not like it?" she asked, shrugging helplessly. "I love it."

"But?" When she glanced at him inquiringly, he added, "I definitely feel there was a 'but' attached to that."

"It's just . . ." She sighed, then said in a rush, "It's just that since it's only temporary I . . . I didn't expect anything like this." She raised her left hand, and the large pink-tinted diamonds circling her finger caught the light and were set afire with dancing sparks.

He laughed softly. "What did you expect? A cigar band?"

"No-o-o, but I didn't think it would be the Sisters of the Kohinoor either." She leaned her head back against his shoulder and frowned. "What if I lose it?"

The amusement was obvious on his face as he smiled down at her and gave her waist a gentle squeeze. "You won't lose it. And even if you did, it's insured. So don't worry." He didn't take his eyes off her, and after a moment he murmured, "Did I tell you how beautiful you look today?"

Turning her head slightly on his shoulder she glanced up at him, and the sight of him took her breath away even more than his lovely ring had. "No," she said, smiling slightly because they both knew he had told her several times. "Tell me."

But he didn't speak. He merely stared at her with a bemused, delighted expression, as though she had done something strange and wonderful by teasing him. After a moment he murmured in a husky voice, "Let's dance," and he led her out onto the small polished dance floor.

She leaned against him, letting him guide her movements as the soft, romantic music floated through the hall. They could have been alone for all the attention they paid to the other people on the dance floor, people who stared with knowing smiles as Jake and Toby waltzed by.

When the lovely music faded away he tilted her chin and studied her pale features. "You're tired," he murmured. "Let's go home, little one."

She had wondered why he had chosen to have the reception at a hotel rather than in his own home. As they made their way past the guests, most of them people from Jake's office, she knew why he had wanted to have the reception at the hotel. It was so that they could leave at any point they desired.

On the ride home, his arm around her made a warm cocoon that soothed away the tiredness, and it was only when they stopped before the door of her new bedroom that the cocoon was lifted along with his arm. It was more of a shock than it really should have been, and she shivered, feeling suddenly cold and bereft.

The whisper of a kiss on her forehead, the searching intensity of his blue eyes on her face, and his softly murmured, "Sweet dreams, wife." Then, as though he savored the words, he said again, "My wife." These things stayed with her as she drifted off to sleep, and they filled her dreams with his presence, making them sweeter than even he could have wished.

But along with the morning mist that disappears and is forgotten with the sun, the dreams were gone.

Toby stretched luxuriously and looked around

this new world of hers. This morning it did seem as though the whole world was new instead of just her corner of it. Oddly enough, the newness didn't frighten her. She felt instead a wonderful exhilaration.

She sat up in the small, single bed and wrapped her arms around her knees. She knew the bed had been purchased especially to make her feel more at home. Her copper alarm clock sat on the nightstand. Her brushes and porcelain powder box were on the mahogany dresser. Snapshots of the children from the hospital decorated the mirror. It had truly become *her* room.

Jumping from the bed, she began to hum under her breath as she washed her face and brushed her teeth, then gave the vanity mirror a foamy grin when she realized she was doing a shaky rendition of "Oh, What a Beautiful Morning."

It was as though new blood were flowing through her veins, she thought as she pulled on her jeans and a mint green sweater. She was filled with a strange excitement . . . and anticipation.

And today for the first time in memory, Toby didn't question the way she felt. She didn't poke and pry and dissect her emotions. She simply laughed aloud in the empty room and went in search of Jake and breakfast . . . and perhaps even adventure. *Who knows?* she thought with a crooked grin.

She didn't have far to look for Jake nor, it seemed, for the adventure. He met her in the hall and gave her a quick, harried look before taking her hand and hurrying her along to the small breakfast room that overlooked the wild tangle of the back yard.

"The aunts called this morning," he said, his voice filled with wary urgency as he poured two cups of coffee. He handed her one and took the seat across from her.

"The ants?" she asked, then the idea caught her imagination and suddenly a vivid picture formed in her mind. The picture was of a cigar-smoking ant with horn-rimmed glasses and bow tie leaning back in his little ant chair to prop his feet on his little ant desk while he talked to Jake on his little ant phone.

"Aren't you leaving enough crumbs out?" she said, propping her chin on her hand to stare at him curiously. "Are they going on strike?" Her dreamy smile widened as the picture grew.

The brave ants marched daily before the residence of Mr. Hammond, defying gusty breezes and rumors that anteaters had been hired as strikebreakers. Their tiny placards never wavered as crowds of grasshoppers and gnats gathered to jeer at the determined marchers.

"Toby!"

Her eyes focused on the exasperation in his face, and she shook her head. "Oh. I'm sorry Jake. Tell me about the ants."

"They want to meet you. Today," he said with resignation. "I had hoped to put it off until you had a chance to settle in, but they insisted."

She stared at him for a moment in silence, then her eyes widened. *"Aunts,"* she said finally as comprehension dawned. "Your *aunts* want to meet me." Then she frowned, and her eyes widened as she gave him a wary look. "Oh . . . Jake, your aunts want to meet me."

"That's what I just said," he said, giving her a confused glance. "It's nothing for you to worry about. They're sweet old darlings, but—"

"But?"

"Maybe it would be better if you met them and

formed your own opinions," he said, then laughed softly. The laugh made her more nervous than anything else.

It took them longer to get away from the house than he had planned because Toby couldn't decide what to wear to meet the aunts. Jake would give her no clue to their personalities, simply telling her that there were two of them, Sophie and Annabelle. In the end she chose a buttercup yellow suit with slim skirt and demure white blouse, but was still not happy with the choice.

She paused in applying a muted beige lipstick and grimaced at the face in the mirror. "It'll be just my luck," she muttered, "if the aunts turn out to be a couple of swinging little old ladies who listen to punk rock and make funny brownies."

But as soon as she saw the residence of Misses Sophie and Annabelle Hammond she knew they were not part of the swinging crowd. The enormous house was blatantly, triumphantly Gothic. However instead of dark, oppressing colors, it had been painted an eye-opening combination of peach and pumpkin.

Before walking through the iron gate that opened to the front walk, Jake paused and grinned down at her. "What do you think so far?"

"I absolutely adore it." She laughed. "It looks like a stage setting for the musical version of *The Fall of the House of Usher*." She smiled up at him, her brown eyes shining with excitement. "I think I'm going to enjoy meeting 'the aunts' very much."

"Suppose we go in and find out," he said briskly, but he couldn't hide the fact that he was pleased with her response, and the look in his eyes sent a slow warmth straight to her heart.

He didn't knock on the front door, but used a key to open it, then ushered Toby inside. He paused as though gauging her reactions. The interior of the extraordinary house was a continuation of the unusual exterior. As the heavy door swung shut behind them and the only light came through the stained glass fan over the door, Toby could just barely make out the impressive curved staircase at the end of the hall and the lone rug that lay before it, reposing in alarming purple splendor.

She stared about her in fascination as Jake glanced into a room that appeared to be a small parlor. She vaguely took in his whispered, "They must be in the study," before he led her along the hall to throw open huge double doors.

There was more light in the room they entered now, and for a moment Toby simply stared in wide-eyed awe. The room seemed to be crammed full of overstuffed furniture in varying shades of brown. Between the massive couches and chairs and chaise longues were innumerable burlwood tables, Japanese screens, and tall thin shelves to hold trinkets from a different era.

In one corner of the room was an object that surely couldn't be anything other than a gold, cupid-adorned harp. Before she could look closer, though, her eyes were caught by the animals that were scattered about the room—a coat rack made of antlers, a huge bird with spread wings that looked vaguely vulturish, a full-size bear that seemed to be guarding the harp, and on the hearth something definitely reptilian that resembled Godzilla.

"Why, doesn't she look sweet, Sister?"

Toby pulled her eyes away from the astounding room and saw what she had missed before. Two tall pink and silver women sat on a loveseat beside a window. They smiled at Toby, then continued with their embroidery.

"Yes . . . sweet," the second aunt replied vaguely. "You wouldn't expect it with Jacob, would you?"

"Now, Sister," the first aunt scolded. "I'm sure Jacob means well. I can't say that his understanding is exactly great, but nevertheless he means well. And in any case it was a long time ago that he painted 'The Foot.' You certainly can't judge him on that alone."

"But he *did* paint it," the second aunt insisted.

Toby regarded Jake with an amusement that threatened to overflow. He often stared at her with that same confused expression that was on his face now, as though he had somehow stumbled into the Mad Hatter's tea party.

Toby crossed the room and sat on a footstool at the aunts' feet. "Whose foot did he paint?" she asked, intrigued.

"Why it was *Papa's*," the first aunt said in horror. "He brought it back from one of his African safaris . . . or was it India. . . . Well, never mind. It was years and years ago when Sister and I were only girls."

"I don't believe, Sister," the second aunt said with genteel indignation, "that you need dwell on how long ago it was that we were girls. Especially since you are the elder. . . ."

"But surely," said the first aunt with a conciliatory smile, "surely, Sister, you're the elder."

"No, I distinctly remember—" the second began stubbornly.

The first aunt patted the second's hand and said, "It doesn't matter. We were both very young when Papa brought home 'The Foot.' And I know it was very naughty of Jacob to paint it orange, but really I saw no need to store it in the attic. It might have looked quite nice filled with pampas grass."

Toby grinned up at Jake as he came to stand

beside her. He shoved his hands into the pockets of his slacks and muttered, "I was eleven." She swallowed a laugh at his disgruntled features, then turned back as the gentle argument proceeded.

"No one has an orange elephant foot," said the second aunt, then bent to continue her embroidery.

"What do you think, dear?" the first asked Toby in her soft, feminine voice.

Toby smiled. "I think an orange elephant foot might be quite . . . interesting."

"The young have no sense of dignity," the second aunt muttered.

"No, no. Now I must protest, Sister," said the first.

Jake bent down and whispered, "Miss Annabelle," as he nodded at the gentle first aunt.

"You can't condemn the young people out of hand," continued Miss Annabelle. "After all, think of Althea Lewis." She turned to Toby. "Althea—"

"Sister!" Miss Sophie scolded. "Surely you're not—No, you can't mean to tell that story. It's too naughty." She paused thoughtfully. "Is Althea dead now?" When Miss Annabelle nodded, her sister smiled for the first time since since the argument began. "Then I don't suppose it matters, does it?"

Miss Annabelle put down her embroidery and clasped Toby's hands, her eyes sparkling with mischievous amusement as she began the story.

"Althea was the head librarian for years, and her entire life was ruled by the factory whistle. She got out of bed when it blew at five in the morning, went to work when it blew at eight, to lunch when it blew at noon, and came home when it blew at five. Finally, after fifty years obeying the dictates of the factory whistle, she retired."

She paused, and both aunts began to giggle girlishly, hiding the sound behind fragile pink hands.

"On the first Monday after her retirement," Miss Annabelle continued, "she heard the whistle blow and jumped out of bed as usual. Then when she realized what she had done she walked out onto her front porch—"

Delighted chuckles were interspersed with speech, and the story continued, each of them interrupting the other to speak.

"—in her *nightdress,* my dear—"

"—then she put her thumb to her nose—"

"—and made a *gesture* at the whistle."

"Imagine Miss Althea Lewis doing a thing like that!"

Toby almost fell off her stool as she laughed with them. She laughed not so much at the story but at the aunt's own laughter and obvious enjoyment of their "naughty" friend.

As the two delightful women served tea in delicate china cups, Toby became more and more captivated by the way their disjointed comments would pop into the conversation, never to be explained by either, but obviously understood by both.

And even as they scolded Jake for holding his teacup improperly, for not bringing Toby to see them before the wedding, and for never eating his broccoli when he was a boy, Toby could see the affection in their eyes, eyes so like Jake's. The love they felt for their nephew showed, not in what they said, but in the way they touched his hair when they passed him, in the way their faces lit up when he spoke to them.

As the morning passed, Toby somehow knew that the aunts' affection was freely being extended to her. She was unfamiliar with such open acceptance and didn't quite know how to react. Luckily, it seemed that no more was expected of her than that she be herself.

It was only as they were leaving that she realized with a startled laugh that although Jake had tried several times, Toby had never been formally introduced to the aunts.

In the car he turned to her and said wryly, "What do you think? They aren't exactly the usual sort of relative."

She finally allowed her amusement full rein. "But then I'm not the usual sort of wife, am I?" she asked, chuckling. "No, I like them very much. They're so . . ." She paused, searching for the right word. "Surreal."

His echoing laugh sounded relieved. "I was afraid you might think the baby was liable to inherit some strange genes."

"If it can get past my strange genes, I'm sure the aunts' will be no problem." She stared out the window for a moment. "They're very loving people, and that's what really matters, isn't it?"

"Yes," he murmured, his voice oddly husky. "I guess it is, at that."

As Toby shifted her position on the loveseat she tried harder to concentrate on her book. It was difficult because she could feel Jake watching her. She knew she should be used to it by now. She and Jake had been married for a month, and in that time he had constantly watched her, sometimes with a thoughtful look on his face, sometimes with an expectant one. She often wondered just what it was he expected her to do.

Toby dear, did you know that daffodils have begun to sprout from the top of your head? It's a little early for them, don't you think?

She smiled and looked up. Finding him watching her just as she had known he would be, she sighed. "Haven't you ever heard that a watched pot never boils?"

"Was I staring again?" he said apologetically. "I don't do it on purpose." He stood and moved across the room to sit beside her. "Did you know that everything you eat and drink goes to the baby?"

She glanced down at the book in his hands and sighed again. If he wasn't watching her, he was reading books about pregnancy.

"Yes, I knew that," she said indulgently, then returned to her book.

He remained silent for a moment, then said stubbornly, "I was just wondering about that medication that Dr. Mathias gave you for depression."

Toby had forgotten all about the medication that had been the cause of her present situation. She put down her book and turned to face him. "Didn't I tell you? As soon as Dr. Mathias and Dr. White realized how sensitive I was to drugs, they took me off them. There was no reason to take unnecessary chances. So the crucial first three months of pregnancy went along without drugs, Jake." She glanced at him with amusement. "Dr. Mathias assures me there couldn't have been any harm done to our baby. Does that make you feel better?"

"Don't laugh at me, Toby," he said, although he was laughing at himself. "I just want to know what's happening."

"I know," she said gently, patting his hand. "You don't want to miss a minute of it."

They both settled back to read again, but very little time had passed before she could feel Jake staring again. She glanced up to tease him, then stopped when she found him staring intently at her legs, which were curled up beside her. Suddenly he reached out slowly, and she watched in fascination as he pressed on her skin with his index finger.

"*Jake,*" she said in exasperation. "What are you doing now?"

"I just wanted to be sure you aren't retaining water," he explained hastily. "The book said too much salt will do that, and you eat a lot of peanuts."

She turned in her seat and clasped his face between her hands. It didn't occur to her that a month ago she would have been petrified to make such a gesture.

"Listen carefully, papa," she said slowly. "I'm fine. The baby's fine. I have two doctors checking constantly on my progress. *You don't have to worry.*"

When he started to protest, she added, "Jake, ninety-four point three percent of the women who eat peanuts have healthier babies. It's all that protein. Now you can't argue with the statistics."

He watched her silently for a moment, then his eyes narrowed suspiciously. "You made that up."

"Of course I did," she admitted smugly. "I always do. I find it not only settles a lot of arguments, but it makes me sound smart." She grinned. "No one ever bothers to look it up."

He threw back his head, and the room was filled with the rich sound of his laughter. Putting his arm around her, he gave her a squeeze as she looked up at him in laughing innocence. "You're wonderful. I promise I'll try to behave. It's just that I can't seem to get it off my mind. It's such an extraordinary thing—the birth of a baby. Even at the office—"

He broke off suddenly and looked at his watch. "Hell, I forgot B.J. was coming by this evening to get some papers." He exhaled in a rough, regretful sigh. "I'd better go get them together."

"B.J.?"

"My assistant," he explained, his mind already switched to business as he leaned down to kiss her nose.

Toby stared after him until he was out of sight. She still couldn't believe the way they had adjusted to each other. In one month they had grown to be friends. She felt as comfortable with Jake as though she had known him forever.

And Janine had been right, she thought with a laugh. Although she teased Jake about watching her, she had come to accept it as a part of him, knowing there was nothing dark and mysterious about the watchfulness.

The part she had not suspected beforehand was the unbelievable care he took with her. It was not only her health as the mother of his unborn child that interested him. He wanted to know everything about her. They spent hours each day talking, never tiring of each other's company, always discovering something new and interesting about the other person.

Yes, his care was something entirely new for her, but she wasn't reticent about accepting it. She absolutely reveled in it.

Toby had had friends before. They had in some ways compensated for her lack of affection at home, but she had never had a friend with whom she felt completely natural. Not until Jake. She hid her fears and dark moods from her other friends, but she could hide nothing from Jake. The extraordinary thing was that she had not once had to fight the debilitating depression since they had been married. It was almost as though her mind had been so full of the baby and her new relationship with its father that there hadn't been room for anything else.

Only one thing was missing from Toby's new life, and since she had never had it she really couldn't say it was missing. Maybe "yearned for" was a better description. The crazy tingling, the heavy-duty closeness she had felt when she and Jake had sat in the closet of her apartment had not happened again. He had been too wonderful for her to complain, but still a little of that kind of thing would make her life complete. She was so new to the business of touching she finally decided that the melting feelings that had come to her on that day must be something friends saved for special occasions.

But every so often when Toby looked at Jake without his knowledge, she wondered if such occasions couldn't be manufactured. She smiled mischievously as she thought of how she had often been tempted to pretend an emotional upset just so she could feel the wonderful sensations his special brand of comforting brought.

Rising from the loveseat, she wandered into the kitchen for a glass of milk, then stepped out onto the patio. It was colder now, and except for the pines most of the trees were bare. Fallen leaves were everywhere, crackling beneath her feet as she strolled contentedly in the early evening air. Through the naked trees she could see to the back of Jake's property. It was larger than it looked at first glance—as she had discovered on her first walk there—and filled with small, surprising spots of beauty that were hidden until one stumbled upon them.

Shivering as a cold breeze whipped through the piles of leaves, she walked around to the door that led from the patio to her bedroom. She needed to get a sweater. When she passed the study window, opened a crack, she heard Jake speaking and smiled at the businesslike tone, then her steps slowed when she heard a woman's voice. It didn't occur to her until later that she was eavesdropping.

"Where's your wife, Jake? I'm curious to know what kind of woman you married. I must say I was disappointed to be away on a business trip and to have to miss the wedding." The soft, feminine voice sounded faintly scolding. "Are you hiding your wife?"

"You sound disapproving," Jake said, amusement in his tone of voice.

"Not disapproving. Distinctly jealous," the woman said lightly. "You know I wanted to marry you myself." Although it sounded like a joke, Toby could hear an element of truth in the woman's words. "I rather fancied being Mrs. President of SGC."

"If you make a few more smart deals like the Jackson one, you won't have to marry for the presidency, B.J. They'll hand it to you on a platter." Jake was all business now.

"Somehow I don't see the board of directors passing over you to offer me the job," B.J. said, laughing ruefully. "I guess I'll have to be satisfied with being your valued assistant."

"Well, you're definitely that." Now he sounded thoroughly bored with the subject and didn't hesitate to change it. "Come and meet Toby. I guarantee it'll be an experience for you."

"I'm intrigued, darling," B.J. said, with what sounded to Toby like superior amusement.

" 'I'm intrigued, dah-ling,' " Toby mimicked nastily, kicking at the green garden hose that was coiled in the grass at the edge of the patio. " 'I rather fancied myself as Mrs. President.' That . . .

that *assistant."* She spat it out as though it were a dirty word.

Toby walked silently into the trees that bordered the patio on the north side, muttering to herself as she walked, never stopping to wonder why the woman disturbed her so much. She only knew that she did, very much indeed. For the first time since she had been with Jake, Toby felt like hiding in the closet. This B.J. sounded so sophisticated, so sure of herself. And although Toby had run into a lot of people like her, for some reason this particular woman bothered her.

Suddenly Toby looked up to find that she had wandered quite a way from the house. Jake would be wondering where she was. She turned and hurried back. She was out of breath and ready to apologize when she walked back into the study, but it was empty.

Hearing voices in the hall, she turned in that direction. When she got to her bedroom she found the door ajar and laid her hand against it to push it open. Glancing around the room, she swallowed a hysterical laugh when she saw Jake opening the closet door as he called her name.

The woman in the room was of average height, but had encased in a tight dress a figure that would make better women than Toby envious. Her lustrous auburn hair caught the light in the room and blazed brightly. Toby strained her eyes trying to find a flaw, but the only thing she could see was unusually thin lips, and a deft hand with the lipstick brush seemed to have taken care of that. B.J. had the market cornered on everything but homely.

She was laughing softly at Jake's peculiar behavior, then glanced speculatively at the single bed where Toby slept. "Does your wife often hide in the closet?" she asked, not bothering to disguise her amusement. "Is she a little . . . strange?"

Toby pushed the door open wider. "Yes, she does," she said casually. "And yes, she is." She extended her hand as she walked into the room. "Hi. I'm Toby, and you must be B.J."

She saw the woman's eyes narrow as she took in Toby's maternity top, but neither of them commented as they shook hands. Turning to Jake, Toby smiled wryly and said, "I'm sorry you couldn't find me. I was walking in the garden."

Jake's expression changed immediately from amusement to concern. "Without a sweater? Toby, it's chilly out there." He walked to her and took both her hands in his. "Toby Hammond! Your hands are freezing. What are you trying to do, catch pneumonia?"

For a moment Toby was struck by the strange look on B.J.'s face. She was looking at Jake as though she had never seen him before, as though his actions were totally out of character.

Then when his arm came around her, Toby smiled up at him, forgetting all about their guest. "I'm fine," she said softly. "I only stayed out for a minute." She leaned her head against him, rubbing her face on the roughness of his chambray shirt. "You've got to stop worrying so much."

As he looked down at her and smiled with her, the strange, restless feelings that had come upon her in the garden disappeared. She had forgotten them completely by the time she and Jake walked his assistant to the door.

When Jake moved away to retrieve her jacket, B.J. turned her attention to Toby, regarding her quizzically. "You're a witch, right?"

When Toby stared at her in bewilderment, the other woman shook her head with a wry smile.

"Never mind. It doesn't matter. I guess I had convinced myself that Jake wasn't capable of more warmth than he showed me." She sighed. "I can see now that I was wrong." Extending her hand, she added, "I'm glad I met you, Toby. It was . . . enlightening, to say the least."

Later that night, Toby lay awake thinking about what B.J. had said and remembering what Lynda had told her about Jake. He wasn't known as a nice man. If anything, he had a reputation for being the opposite. That didn't make sense. Jake was the warmest, nicest person she had ever met. Could everyone else be wrong about him? Or was it simply that he was different when he was with her?

There was no way for Toby to know for sure without asking someone who had known him intimately before their marriage, but from what she had seen and heard, that person didn't seem to exist.

Jake's rare comments about his first marriage told her his relationship with his ex-wife had not been close. He merely said they didn't understand each other and had found communication difficult, but his face had been cold when he spoke of that time, reminding Toby of her first encounter with him—before she had met the man behind the mask.

Even the aunts didn't seem to recognize the softer side of Jake, although it was obvious they loved him. And since both his parents were dead, there seemed to be no one to ask.

Jake was never particularly reluctant to talk about his past. Rather it was as though there was nothing that interested him enough to talk about. He seemed much more interested in Toby and her past and, sometimes, her future.

As the days passed, Toby forgot to worry about

how other people saw Jake. She was too absorbed in preparing for the arrival of the baby and basking in the warmth of Jake's care.

They laughed a lot when they were together—at each other and at the world that would receive their child. They seemed to discover something new in each other, and in the world, with each passing day. And the changes in Toby, emotionally as well as physically, escaped her notice, but were carefully noted and stored away by the ever watchful Jake. He didn't know himself what he was waiting for, he only knew that he was and that it would turn out to be important in his life.

A month after B.J.'s visit, Jake smiled over at Toby as he drove to a concert they had both been looking forward to. He stifled a chuckle when he saw her hands resting comfortably on the swell beneath her filmy green dress. Toby had grown in more ways than one in the two months they had been married.

Suddenly she inhaled sharply with a surprised, "Oh!"

His eyes narrowed in concern, and he quickly pulled the car over to the side of the street. "What is it? What's wrong?" he said anxiously, bending over her.

She didn't speak. She picked up his large hand and placed it where her own rested on her abdomen. He stared at her questioningly for a moment, then miraculously he felt a strong jab against his hand.

He caught his breath, his eyes widening, then suddenly he began to laugh. A rich, strong laugh. A laugh of exploding joy. And she laughed with him, at the healthy life within her and—maybe—at his pleasure in that life.

Closing his eyes tightly, Jake leaned his head

down until it rested against the soft swell of her breasts. As her hand came up to cradle his face, he felt a vibrant warmth well up inside him. The struggle to contain it took a great effort on his part, but after a while he blinked away the unfamiliar moisture in his eyes and pulled again onto the street.

Neither of them was aware that in the moments they had sat pressed together they hadn't spoken a word. The communication between them had been sharp and clear, as if they had been thinking with one mind.

As he drove, Jake could still feel his heart pounding strangely. More and more the wonder he felt at the idea of having a child of his own was mingling and becoming one with his wonder in the woman beside him. He had thought Toby attractive the first time he had seen her. Now he knew she was the most beautiful woman he had ever known.

Toby believed he watched her because he was worried about the baby, he thought with a self-mocking smile. He didn't know how she would react if she knew that he was fascinated as much by her as he was by the baby.

As they walked from the car park to the concert hall, he found himself watching her again from the corners of his eyes. She had the strange faraway expression on her face that appeared too often for his peace of mind.

"Toby," he said softly, then more insistently, *"Toby."* She blinked and shook her head slightly, then looked up at him questioningly. "Where do you go when you leave Earth?" he asked wryly.

"I beg your pardon?"

"Every so often you go away and I feel I should make a long-distance call to reach you."

"Oh," she said, laughing. "I talk to myself in my head."

"Talk to me instead."

She glanced up at him doubtfully. "I don't think—" she began, but his determined stare stopped her. She shrugged as if to say, "Okay, you asked for it."

"Say, George—" she said.

"George? George who?"

She stopped walking. "Do you want to hear this or not?" He nodded, swallowing his laugh, and she continued. "Say George, look who's coming. It's that good looking Jake Hammond and his wife the eighteen-wheeler."

Jake's laugh caught the attention of the other people on their way to the concert. He put his arm around Toby and gave her a swift hug. "You're the most beautiful, fascinating eighteen-wheeler I've ever seen."

And it was the truth, he thought as they continued walking. What was also the truth, but what he knew not to say aloud, was that she was also the sexiest eighteen-wheeler he had ever seen.

He looked down at her as they walked through the high glass doors of the concert hall and added huskily, "You're the most beautiful woman here."

"Oh, yeah?" she said skeptically, then nodded to a group of people on their right. "What about her?"

Jake looked at the tall, slender blonde that Toby had indicated and studied her silently for a moment. His eyes grew reflective before he turned back to Toby. "She's very attractive," he said truthfully. "But there's something missing." His voice was thoughtful as he tried to pinpoint what was wrong with the seductively dressed woman. "I can't put my finger on it. There's just something missing."

"About thirty pounds, I'd say," Toby said dryly. "And half of her dress."

Toby always made him laugh. Not always at what she said, but just the way she said it, the expressions on her face as she absorbed the confusing world around them. He hadn't realized how much laughter was missing from his life until he had met her. They were still laughing on the drive home after the concert when she began to give him a perfect imitation of the very-much-married couple that had sat in the seats directly in front of their own.

About halfway through the drive home, she paused and yawned, reminding him of a lazy cat as she covered her small mouth.

"Here," he said pulling her across the seat. "Lean on me and stop fighting it. You're exhausted."

"I can't understand why I sleep so much," she murmured groggily as she leaned against him.

"You're sleeping for two now," he said, but she didn't hear. She had fallen asleep almost as soon as her head dropped to his chest.

He felt the warmth of her beside him, and as they neared the house he slowed the car, reluctant to have that warmth removed. But he couldn't put it off forever, and all too soon he pulled the car into the circular drive and parked in front of the house.

He looked down at her for a moment, then stepped from the car and lifted her into his arms, smiling because even in her present state she still weighed no more than the average woman. He gained a few extra minutes as he waited for Mrs. Pratt to open the door, then he moved past his housekeeper with a silent nod and walked to Toby's bedroom.

As he lay her on her bed, he glanced back to see if Mrs. Pratt had followed them, but the hall was empty. Of course, he thought with a sigh. She had naturally thought Jake would take care of getting his wife to bed.

Staring down at Toby, he felt his mouth go inexplicably dry. He stood beside the bed for a moment, then reached out slowly. But when he saw how much his hand trembled, he jerked it back and wheeled away from the bed, running both hands through his hair in exasperation.

"This is ridiculous," he muttered hoarsely. He couldn't just leave her like that. Setting his jaw in hard lines, he moved purposely back to the bed. He eased Toby onto her side, then held her in place with his knee as he lowered the zipper of the filmy green dress. It seemed to take forever, but at last he managed to accomplish the simple task. He let her fall gently on her back again and began to slide the fabric over her shoulders.

Jake didn't notice that his breathing was growing labored and harsh as he tried to keep his mind off the soft warmth of the body beneath his hands, but he couldn't ignore the way his fingers shook and his senses reeled when he pulled the dress below her breasts.

Through the lace bra he could see the creamy swell of her breasts, the darker circles of her nipples, and he held his breath, his facial muscles tightening into a painful grimace. He was terrified that the frustrated groan building deep inside him would awaken her.

For a long time he stood frozen, staring down at the pale loveliness that lay before him, so like that night five months ago. He fought it—God! how he fought it—but inevitably his mind was taken over by the memory of the sight and feel and scent of her.

Erotic scenes held him enthralled. Scenes of

Toby pulling his head to her breast, of Toby wrapping her slim legs around him. Toby, always Toby, so sweet, so loving. He could almost taste her warm flesh on his tongue.

He had no control over the hand that reached out to caress her breast through the thin lace. The nipple hardened immediately beneath his touch, and no thoughts of how he was violating her privacy came to stop him from sliding his hand beneath the lace to cup one full breast.

As if in a trance, he leaned over until he caught the scent of her flesh and could feel her warmth reaching out to him, pulling him ever closer.

Then suddenly Toby sighed in her sleep, stirring slightly. Jake jerked his hand back as though he had been burned and spun away, closing his eyes in frustration.

What in hell did he think he was doing? he asked himself in disgust. Toby trusted him. How could he break that trust? He had no right. Dammit, he had no right.

But even the tremendous heat of his anger couldn't hide the more intense heat that raged in his loins. He wanted Toby with a deep, burning hunger. The desire he had felt on that memorable night had grown until it was now almost out of control. He lived constantly with the fear that he couldn't limit his caresses to the casual ones she seemed to prefer.

Glancing back at her over his taut shoulder, he pulled his face into grim lines as he made the decision to get Mrs. Pratt's help, leaving her to draw her own conclusions.

But before he could leave the room, Toby stirred again. As he turned back to her, her eyelids lifted slightly and she smiled, a slow, achingly sensual smile, as she had on another unforgettable night.

Then without waking fully she sighed and curled over on her side.

Jake's knuckles showed white as he clenched his fists into tight balls, and he felt his stomach twist up in hard knots of need. His movements were strangely mechanical as he walked slowly out of her bedroom, feeling a deep well of loneliness overwhelm him.

Seven

Toby peered around the door, and when Janine waved her into the airy office, she moved across the room to sit in the familiar chair that had held her on so many visits before.

As she waited for Janine to get off the telephone, Toby shifted her weight uncomfortably, smoothing down the fine woolen fabric of her purple maternity smock. For over eight months—from fall into winter, then into the first struggling green of spring—she had carried the baby easily. However in the last week she had noticed a dramatic change, a pressing heaviness that made every movement an effort.

Clasping her hands beneath her stomach and hoisting slightly to lighten the load, she studied Janine as the other woman spoke quietly into the blue phone. Toby hadn't visited her analyst since before her marriage to Jake. All these months had passed so quickly. She'd been totally absorbed in preparations for the baby. And she had been completely absorbed with Jake. Her days had been filled with baby beds and the guidelines for the safest car seats. Her evenings had been filled most recently with Lamaze classes . . . and from the beginning with Jake.

She smiled now as she thought of Jake and those classes—evenings spent listening to a bubbly, blond instructor and learning more than she ever wanted to know about enemas. The classes were interesting, but the way Jake acted you would think they were meetings of the United Nations General Assembly. Like a sponge, he absorbed every word, then discussed it endlessly afterward.

Toby grinned suddenly when she thought of his enthusiasm. Jake considered any time a good time to practice the breathing and relaxation methods they were learning. Every time she thought he had forgotten for a while and she could relax, he would jump up and approach her with a fervent look in his eyes that Toby was sure would have been familiar to the Salem women accused of witchcraft. It was as though theirs was the first baby ever conceived, as though a king were in the making.

In the last few months the natural hesitancy of a new friendship had mellowed into a comfortable familiarity. Toby knew now that when his favorite ashtray was out of place Jake became irritable, and he knew that she never spent less than an hour in the bathroom.

Every morning she found him at the breakfast table, frowning at the morning newspaper, but when she walked into the room he would lay it aside and smile, greeting her with a teasing remark or a burst of enthusiastic conversation, as though he had saved the beginning of his day for her.

He was such a special person, she thought with a wistful sigh. A special friend. But there were times when she felt that there was something going on inside his head that he took special pains to hide from her. Several times when she had felt him watching her, she had glanced up to catch the oddest expression on his face. It bothered her. While she couldn't say absolutely that it was pain or frustration or tension, it was definitely a strong emotion, and he was definitely trying to hide it from her. As soon as he knew she was watching the mask would come down, and it would be a few uneasy minutes before they regained their normal, easy relationship.

Rubbing her stomach unconsciously, she smiled ruefully. Maybe, like herself, Jake was just beginning to get anxious for the birth of the baby.

"Well, Toby, it's been quite a while."

Toby glanced up as Janine spoke and gave her a grin. "And I'll bet your days have been deadly dull without the 'Terrible Turmoils of Toby' to keep you going."

Janine laughed. "I have to admit you are one of my most unusual patients." She leaned back in her chair. "So how are things with you? Is there a problem with your new life?"

"No, not really." Toby sighed, shaking her head. "It's just that lately I've been feeling . . . well, itchy. I know part of it is waiting for the baby to come, but part of it has to do with Jake."

"Something about your relationship worries you?" Janine asked quietly, beginning the familiar ritual of question and answer.

"It doesn't worry me, exactly. It's more that I simply don't know what our relationship means." She shifted her position again. "It seems that when we're together I'm always expecting something to happen. I don't even know what it is that I expect. I only know that whatever it is it never happens." She gave a short laugh. "It's like trying to remember a word. You know that it's right there on the tip of your tongue, but it just won't come rolling out." She leaned forward. "I feel like there's something I should know that I'm just too stupid to see." She sighed and shook her head. "It's just so frustrating, Janine."

"I see," Janine murmured.

"Well, I don't!" Toby chuckled, then shrugged. "But I suppose I will in time." She glanced up, and her humor grew, her eyes sparkling with amusement. "What is wrong with me? I can't even worry properly anymore. I'm like a placid cow—nothing bothers me as long as I've got a green field and a warm stall."

"I've heard pregnancy does that to you," Janine said, laughing with her. "At least for some women. For others it seems to be a time when all the fears that have been buried in the back of their minds come to the fore. I'm glad that's not the case with you."

Toby kept a smile on her face as she subjected the other woman to a probing stare. "You know, Janine, I believe I've done you an injustice."

"Oh?"

Toby twirled a brown curl around her finger, unsure of how honest she should be. "It's always seemed to me that you were too belligerent as a female and as a professional, as though you were daring someone to separate the two. But lately . . . well, I've been giving it some thought and I believe that maybe I was allowing my own inadequacies to color my view of you. I thought you wanted me to say, 'I am woman, hear me roar,' when all I could manage was, 'I am woman, hear me mumble—but only if it doesn't bother you too much.' "

Janine gave a sputtering laugh of surprise. "And now what do you think?"

Toby smiled. "Now I'm convinced that all you ever wanted me to say was simply, 'I'm Toby,' without excusing myself to anyone—especially myself."

Janine closed her eyes as she rested her head against the high back of her navy leather chair. Then opening her eyes she said quietly, "Toby, you've grown." She gave a husky laugh. "It's almost like having a child leave for college. I feel a little sad, but also very, very proud."

Toby ran her hand through her hair, a little embarrassed by the praise. "Lyell said the same when I met him in the park this morning. First when he looked at my stomach, then later when he had looked at my mind." She paused. "I hadn't thought of it before, but you know, I feel different. I don't spend all my time focusing on myself like I used to. When I have time to sit and reflect on life, it's all directed to Jake and the baby . . . and sometimes the future."

"The future?" Janine asked carefully. "What's in the future for you, Toby? I'm not speaking as your analyst, but as a curious friend. Did you and Jake decide how long you will stay together after the baby is born?"

Toby gave her a startled glance. "After the baby is born? No, no we've never talked about it. We're always too busy talking about the baby and each other. . . . I guess we just forgot about that." She frowned. "It seemed far in the future when everything else was so *immediate.*"

Toby fell into a deep, pensive silence as she stared out the window. "I suppose," she said finally as she looked at Janine with a small, lopsided smile, "that I had better start paying some attention to the future."

And pay attention to the future she did. The drive home passed by in a blur of thought. The afternoon dwindled into evening, and she was still thinking. For once she barely noticed that Jake was watching her as she sat rubbing her chin and biting her lip. She might have spent a lot longer rubbing her chin if she hadn't glanced up just as Jake stood and began walking toward where she sat on the sofa.

"Oh no, Jake," she said warily when she saw the look in his eyes, but he kept walking. "Jake," she pleaded, "if we keep practicing we'll be bored with the whole thing by the time the baby decides to be born." She stood up and started to move away, holding up her hand to stop him. "Personally, I've always thought these things should have some spontaneity."

He gave a snort of laughter as he stopped in front of her.

"Listen, Jake," she said, giving it one last try. "The statistics say—"

"Oh no!" He laughed. "I'm not falling for that again. I know where you get your statistics, remember?"

"No, honest—"

"Come on, I'll help you lie down on the floor," he said, grabbing her hands.

She rolled her eyes in exasperation, but allowed him to lower her to the floor as she muttered under her breath.

"What was that?" he asked, grinning. "I'm afraid I didn't catch that."

"I said," she said between gasps for breath, "that if I lie on the floor many more times it will straighten out the natural curvature of my spine.

Not to mention what it's doing to the curves in my rear."

"Your derriere is as gorgeous as always," he said, chuckling.

"Really?" She tried to roll sideways to get a glimpse of the part of her anatomy in question, but gave it up with a breathless groan when her body refused to twist in that particular direction.

"Take my word for it," he said, pushing her gently back to the floor. "Now start panting while I rub your tummy."

She raised a hand to object further, then suddenly gasped, "Oh my heavens!"

"What is it?" he asked anxiously, leaning over her. "Are you all right? Does something hurt?"

She didn't hear the fear in his voice as she stared at her hand in disgust. "Look," she said, moving her hand so he could see. "I broke a nail. Do you know how long it's taken me to grow these? And it's the first time I've ever had long—"

"Toby, you fiend," he said, rocking back to sit on his heels. "You scared the hell out of me."

"Well, it's not *that* bad," she said, her voice puzzled. "It'll grow back."

He closed his eyes and took a deep breath, then said quietly, "Pant, Toby."

"Jake," she said after a few minutes. "Have you ever thought how ridiculous we would look if someone walked in on us?"

He didn't pause as his hands moved over her abdomen. "Who's going to walk in except Mrs. Pratt? And even if they did, it's not ridiculous."

"A woman lying on the floor panting while a man rubs her stomach is not ridiculous?" she asked dryly between pants. "It not only sounds ridiculous, it sounds downright kinky."

The movements of his hands stopped momentarily as he gave a spurt of surprised laughter. "Kinky?" he asked. "What do you know about kinky?" He shifted his position. "Now practice blowing."

"You think—" She blew out for several seconds. "—that I don't know about things like that?" When he gave her a stern look, she blew out in frustration. After a moment, she paused again. "I've never eaten raw fish either, but I bet I'd recognize it if I saw it."

"Blow," he ordered. "And I'm not questioning your intelligence. I was just surprised."

She propped herself up on her elbows. "I'll bet I think of a lot of things that would surprise you."

"Such as?"

"Such as the plan you talked them into trying at SGC," she said smugly. "Lynda told me all about it. It makes sure that management treats the workers like the Japanese do, emphasizing how important they are to the company and that the company really belongs to them too. I think you did the right thing."

He smiled. "I'm glad you think so. Is this a subtle way of telling me that you would like for me to start talking to you about my work?"

"I skipped Subtle in school, but I would like to talk about it sometime," she murmured, then eyed him hopefully. "We could start now."

But he wouldn't relent, and the rest of the evening was spent in Lamaze practice. She had managed to forget about her session with Janine for a while, but as soon as she was alone in her bedroom, all the questions returned.

Now it seemed incredible that she could have lived with him this long without thinking of when it would all end. She had known from the beginning that she would eventually return to her apartment. Why did that suddenly bring a cold sensation to the pit of her stomach?

She told herself she wouldn't be losing anything. She would see Jake frequently when he came to visit the baby. Their friendship would continue. . . . What more did she want, for heaven's sake?

But as she pulled on her white satin gown she admitted that she wanted a lot more. Seeing Jake occasionally was simply not enough. Too many things had passed between them, they had shared too much to dismiss their relationship as a casual one after the baby was born.

Sitting on the edge of her bed, she thought of Jake's tenderness, his constant care. Surely that meant something . . . something special.

Then she stood up abruptly as an uncomfortable idea occurred to her. He had told her at the beginning how much having this baby meant to him. It showed in everything he did, everything he said. Given those strong emotions, wouldn't he have treated any woman the way he treated Toby . . . any woman who was carrying his child?

Of course he would have, she told herself unhappily as she paced beside her bed. She began unconsciously rubbing her swollen stomach as a slow, nagging ache began in her back and spread to her lower abdomen. He would have done exactly that. He was that kind of man.

She couldn't leave the thought alone as she moved back and forth in the quietness of her room. She was unable to find a single action of Jake's in the last five months that couldn't be attributed to his desperate need for a child.

She was biting her lip to hold back the tears that shone in her eyes as she finally faced the fact that all the tenderness, all the care had been for the baby. And although she couldn't find it in herself to be jealous of her own child, Toby felt more lost and lonely than she had in her loneliest childhood years.

Leaning against the heavy, mahogany bedpost, she wiped the tears away with fingers that trembled. "Come on, Toby," she whispered. "You're grown now. Janine said so. Lyell said so. You can't stand here worrying about it. *Do* something."

She would simply have to find out what he had planned for the future, then deal with it. She hesitated for a moment, running her hands absent-mindedly over her satin-covered abdomen as the nagging ache grew stronger. Then drawing in a deep breath she turned and walked to the door.

Jake rolled over in the bed restlessly, then muttered, "To hell with it," under his breath. Moving jerkily, he sat up and lit a cigarette before walking to the window.

Nights were the worst, he thought as he leaned against the wall. When the sun was out he could pretend that just being with Toby, being considered a close friend by her, was enough. But when he was forced to retreat to the emptiness of his bedroom, he knew it was a lie.

How could he ever have thought that he could let her go? The idea was inconceivable now. He wanted Toby with him for the rest of his life. He wanted to wake up with her in the mornings; he wanted to feel her next to him at night.

Clenching his fists, he swore viciously under his breath. He should have held on to her that first night and never let her go. But that night had been purely physical. It was only when he came to know her better, when he came to know the real Toby, that he fell totally, irrevocably in love with her.

He smiled. It felt good to admit to himself finally that he loved her. Resting his foot on the window seat, he flexed his tired muscles, his bare back and shoulders gleaming bronze in the moonlight.

Toby fascinated him. She was like a spring morning, changing moods and faces constantly. At first she had been to him like an unfamiliar piece of machinery. He had probed and poked, trying to see how it worked. Then slowly he had come to know the depth of her. He had seen the beauty of her heart and mind. And he had seen the strength and character that even she didn't know she possessed.

Stabbing out his cigarette, he realized he would have to tell her what he wanted from her. He would have to tell her that he wanted their marriage to be real. And he would have to tell her now, before the baby came. Afterward she would naturally start thinking about moving back to her apartment. And he would be damned if he'd let that happen. He needed her too much. There were even times when he told himself that she needed him.

Before he could formulate a plan in his mind, Jake heard a noise behind him and swung around as Toby walked into his bedroom.

"Jake, we need to talk about how long I'm going to stay after the—"

She broke off suddenly. As she stepped forward, the moonlight struck her full in the face. Her shoulders shone pale in the ethereal light, her breasts large and swollen beneath the low-cut satin gown. All this he took in at a glance. But his gaze was caught and held by her face. As she stared at him with a curious intensity, her features had the dazed look of a sleepwalker.

He held his breath in the tense silence, then after

what seemed like hours, she murmured faintly, "The bronze statue."

Moving hesitantly across the room, he stopped directly in front of her. "Toby?" he whispered.

For a moment she stared at his face and his bare chest with a bemused expression, as though she were trying to pull something out of her memory.

"It was you," she whispered at last, her eyes wide with amazement. "Of course it was you."

Jake swallowed a groan, as she slowly reached out to touch his face, but when she slid her hand down to his chest, he couldn't hold it back. The groan came out as a long, rumbling moan. He caught her hand, pressing it close, then pulled her into his arms.

Holding her this close was too much for even Jake's level-headed good sense, and he had no control over his actions as he buried his face in her neck, breathing in the scent of her warm flesh.

"Sweet hell, Toby," he whispered hoarsely. "You make me crazy." Then lowering his head, he covered her lips hungrily with his own, seeking the sweetness that had been denied him so long.

Toby pressed closer. The crazy tingling was starting again, building to heart-shaking quakes. And with it came the sensations she remembered from the last time, the sensations she had longed to experience again. But this time something new had been added. She felt an awareness, a knowledge that hadn't been present before. She wanted, wanted . . .

Suddenly Toby stiffened as a pain gripped her with sharp immediacy.

"What is it?" he asked, his eyes narrowing as he lifted his head.

She shook her head. "I don't know," she murmured. "Some kind of weird cramp."

He held her away from him to give her stomach a worried glance. "Not the baby?"

"No . . . no, it can't be. I can still feel it moving." She grimaced as the pain became stronger. "How long are the first contractions supposed to last, Jake?"

"Thirty to sixty seconds," he said, his voice grim.

Relaxing with a sigh as the pain slid away, she said, "They're lasting longer than that. It must be something else." She turned slightly, then gasped as the pain came back full force and she felt that gravity was pulling at her insides.

"Not another one?" Jake asked, a harsh urgency showing in his voice. When she nodded slowly, he stared at her incredulously. "But you can't." He moved her to the bed, forcing her to sit down, then began to pace. "Dammit, Toby, you can't have the baby now!" he said, almost shouting as though he could force nature to stop until he was better prepared.

She looked up at the impotent frustration in his strong face and said stubbornly in her best Katharine Hepburn voice, "*Never*theless."

"All right." His voice was distracted, his fists clenching and unclenching. "All right. Just stay calm."

"Yes, Jake," she said meekly, hiding a smile.

"We've got to call the doctor," he said, sounding strangely as though he was out of breath. "Is your bag packed?"

Toby nodded, then looked behind him when she saw Mrs. Pratt standing in the open doorway.

"Is anything wrong, Mrs. Hammond?"

"We think maybe the baby is coming," Toby said wryly. "But we're not really sure what to do about it."

"We are very sure what to do," Jake corrected

her. "We're going to the hospital now. Mrs. Pratt, would you get Toby's suitcase from her room?"

"But Jake," Toby protested, "I've got to get dressed, and I wanted to take a shower—" Toby stopped speaking abruptly as another pain took her by surprise, doubling her over.

"Call the doctor, Mrs. Pratt," Jake ordered as he reached down to scoop Toby into his arms. "Tell him we're on our way." He paused to pick up Toby's suitcase before he carried her out to the car.

Toby wasn't sure how long the drive to the hospital took. The pains were no longer separated by pauses, but came in an unbroken stream, and at some time she could remember gripping Jake's arm to gasp, "It's happening too fast, Jake. . . . I'm scared. Something's wrong."

She didn't hear all of what he said to her then, but she felt his arm tighten around her and knew he repeated over and over, "I'm here, sweetheart. It'll be all right. . . . It *has* to be."

Toby viewed the flurry of activity at the hospital through a red haze of pain. She listened to the nurse long enough to know that although such a quick progression of the stages of labor was unusual in a first pregnancy, her baby was fine and on his way.

For the next two hours the intensity of the contractions grew to unbearable proportions and took all her concentration. She lay in a small, brightly lit room with Jake beside her, massaging her abdomen and urging her to pant.

It wasn't supposed to be like this, she thought feverishly. She couldn't seem to get on top of the contractions to ride with them. When she groaned uncontrollably as the pain ripped through her, she revived enough to almost laugh as she heard Jake swearing at a nurse who didn't move fast enough to suit him. The pain was like nothing she had ever felt before, as though her whole body were in the grip of a giant vise that persisted in squeezing her tighter and tighter.

Toward the end of the two hours, she looked up into the unfamiliar sternness of Jake's face. "Jake," she gasped, gripping his hands tightly. "Who was it who told us the contractions would be like menstrual cramps?"

"I don't know, love." He mopped her forehead with a damp towel and repeated in a rough, distracted voice, "I don't know."

"Remind . . ." She paused, unable to hold back a whimper. "Remind me to find out so I can strangle her."

She didn't hear his reply. The next time she managed to get a grip on reality was when she felt the harsh light of the delivery room prying its way through her closed eyelids. The pain had disappeared and a numbness had taken over her body. When she opened her eyes, Jake was at her head, bathing her face and this time instructing her to blow. He looked strange, almost frightened, as he leaned his face close to hers.

Suddenly he caught his breath, then framed her face with his hands to turn her eyes to the mirror above them. "Look," he whispered hoarsely.

As they watched together, the head emerged, then the doctor eased out the full length of the baby. A baby boy, his tiny hands vigorously fighting the very air around him.

"Oh, Jake," Toby said, laughing and crying at the same time. "It's a boy. It's a beautiful boy."

She tried to say more, to tell him how she felt, but she could barely talk for the wild kisses that landed all over her face to the accompaniment of the lovely sounds of their son's healthy cries. Then when Jake moved to rest his face against hers and she felt his tears mingling with hers, she was afraid her heart would burst with the intensity of her joy.

Eight

Toby ran her hand over the amazing flatness of her stomach. Her son was two days old, and she still found it strange that she could turn over and sit up without a struggle, without the mountain in her middle.

Smiling like a contented cat, her thoughts turned—as they invariably did—to her son. She and Jake had decided to name him Adam . . . because he was a first for both of them and because his creation had been a miracle.

He was adjusting to his new environment belligerently, she thought with a rueful grin. Her son was not a placid, cuddly baby who calmly accepted the schedules of the hospital staff. He was the stuff of which revolutionaries were made, demanding with his angry cries that the people around him adjust to his schedule instead of imposing their own.

Toby glanced up as the door opened. When she

saw Lyell walk in, she cautiously pulled herself upright, a welcoming smile on her face.

Her dapper looking friend stood in the middle of the room, looking down his majestic nose at the sterile surroundings, then said, "I've seen the young king, my dear, and I must say I expected to see the queen mother surrounded by royal purple at the very least. I can't say that I like this"—he waved a hand at the room in disgust—"this oatmeal decor."

She laughed. "It's supposed to be soothing, I believe. I'm pretty sure that boring was not the official plan for the place."

"So," he said, sitting in the chair beside her bed to take her hand, "how are you, young Toby? You look very pleased with yourself for having produced that great, strapping boy."

"Isn't he gorgeous?" she asked complacently.

"I would have said that he's remarkably ugly, but I guess one has to make allowances for maternal love."

"Ugly!" she exclaimed. "Lyell, how can you say that? He's the most beautiful baby in the nursery."

"Isn't that rather like saying he's the finest operatic soprano in Oshkosh?" he asked dryly. "Each one of them bears an amazing resemblance to an anemic prune."

Finding herself torn between amusement and indignation, Toby finally gave way to the former in a spurt of laughter.

"Now enough of the new generation," he said. His voice was stern, but his eyes twinkled merrily. "Are you as happy as you look?"

"Do I look ecstatic? Wildly contented? Alive as I've never been?" When he smiled and nodded at her exuberance, she added, "Then I guess I'm as happy as I look."

His fingers made a peak that held his gaze as he spoke slowly. "And it's all due to the new arrival?"

She stared in bewilderment at his long, thin fingers, then glanced up to find him watching her curiously. "No . . . I guess that's only part of it. Jake . . ." She paused, wondering how she could explain about Jake and what he had given her in the time she had been with him. "Jake is a part of it too," she said with a helpless shrug.

"You love this man?"

"Love him?" she asked, frowning as she turned the idea over in her mind. "He's gotten closer to me than anyone else I know. I can talk to him about things I've never talked of before." She smiled. "And even when we don't talk, I just like being with him. Yes, I love him. But that's not the same as being in love with him." She paused, then added quietly, "I don't think I was meant to have that kind of thing."

"You don't?" Lyell stared at her thoughtfully for a few seconds as he stroked his elegant mustache, then said quietly, "Toby, how would you feel if you never saw him again?"

As his question sunk in she froze in startled reaction, then suddenly her heart began to pound painfully in her chest. It felt as though a giant hand were squeezing her and her heart was fighting to sustain its beat.

"Is that it, Lyell?" she whispered. "Is that what it feels like to be in love?"

"I'm afraid it is, my dear."

"But how could I not know?" She sat up straighter, then winced when she felt the stitches pull. Suddenly she slapped the bed in disgust, her small face coming alive as she considered this new idea. "I'm so *dumb*," she muttered in irritation, running a hand through her hair. "How could something like that happen without my being aware of it? I thought love was something that came on you all of a sudden. Isn't it supposed to hit you like a ton of bricks?"

"Not always." He reached over to pat her hand in a gesture of comfort. "Sometimes it sneaks up on you, taking over bits and pieces of you until one day you look up and the whole of you is given over to love." He smiled. "It's certainly not something to get upset about."

Lyell paused as though carefully weighing his words, then said, "Toby, have you talked to Jake about . . . about how long you're going to stay with him now that the baby is here?"

She gave him a nervous glance. Lyell didn't usually tiptoe around a subject, and she found she didn't like it at all when he did. It made her extremely nervous.

"I was trying to bring up the subject when my labor pains began," she whispered, feeling a strange fear grow inside her.

"So what are you going to do now that you know that you're in love with him?"

"What can I do?" She shrugged, and her voice was sadder than she knew when she continued. "I want to stay forever, but I'll have to do whatever is right for Jake. You told me that yourself. You said you can never be happy at someone else's expense." She stared at her hands on the bed. "Loving him means I have an obligation to him . . . just like the obligation I have to Adam. Any decision I make has to be based on what is right for him."

Lyell was silent for a moment. "You were a lovely, winsome child, Toby, but now it seems you've become a lovely, mature woman. Your Jake doesn't know how lucky he is."

Lucky, she thought unhappily after Lyell left. Lucky to be loved by an A number-one, genuine nothing. Lucky to become entangled with a woman who was twenty-three years old and could not list one single accomplishment to her name.

Thoughts of Adam and the children she had worked with before her marriage intruded momentarily, but even they couldn't overcome her dark thoughts. Adam wasn't something for which she had planned and worked. Like everything else in her life, he had just happened.

Her position at the day care center had been filled very easily when she left. Anyone who loved children could do it. And her work with handicapped children—as much as it gave to her—didn't really give the children all that much, an occasional laugh maybe or a weekend treat, but nothing substantial . . . such as a new start in life.

"I should have an occupation," she murmured, staring at the ceiling. How could she expect Jake to care about her when until now she hadn't really cared about herself?

She had dropped out of college after the first year because of being thrown in with all those hungry young men. And even though she had immediately begun to work with underprivileged and handicapped children, she brought nothing to her work except enthusiasm. Any real problem had to be handled by the experts. Why had she never considered training for the work she loved so much?

She sighed and closed her eyes. She knew why. She had been a scared little girl—afraid to venture into the world outside her comfortable eggshell, afraid of being hurt, afraid to take a chance on life. She was the seed curled up in the warm, comforting earth. But she had remained dormant long after nature had intended, and sooner or later she would have begun to deteriorate.

It hurt to remember what she had been like then. When had she become dissatisfied with that kind of life? Was it Adam who had made the difference?

Carrying Adam, being responsible for another human being certainly had made a difference, but she knew that wasn't why she had changed. The change had begun the day she had allowed Jake into her life. He had made opening up to life worth taking a chance on. He had shown her that the best that life had to offer was available to her. And even when she was no longer his wife, she would never be able to go back to what she was. The world lay before her now. She was still afraid, but that wouldn't keep her from living.

And it wouldn't keep her from doing everything in her power to make Jake fall in love with her. She couldn't wait around to see what life threw at her, not this time. His love was too important. It wouldn't just fall into her lap. It was something she had to earn, and that was just what she would try to do. Then if he still wanted her to leave at least she would know that she had tried to do something, that she had tried to control her life.

The opening of the door to her room broke into her deep thoughts, and she looked up expectantly. She held back a disappointed frown as Lynda walked in.

"Toby!" Lynda said in bubbling enthusiasm. "He's the most gorgeous thing I've ever seen." She grinned. "I want one too."

"I could get Dr. Mathias to prescribe some antidepressants for you," Toby said, smiling in response to Lynda's enthusiastic expression.

Lynda laughed. "I don't think it would work for me. My metabolism is different. Nothing affects me. Besides, I think I'd rather know when my baby was conceived."

"Yes, I know what you mean," Toby murmured, wishing that she had that memory at least to hold on to.

Lynda sat down beside her and handed her a brightly wrapped package. "For Adam," she said, then gestured to the flowers lining the room. "Are you going into the florist business for yourself?"

Toby laughed shyly. "Jake overdid it just a little. He's very proud of his son."

"And who can blame him?" Suddenly Toby's friend began to giggle, and the sound was slightly malicious.

"What's the giggle for?"

"I was just thinking what it would have been like if Harry—whose last name by the way is Perkins— had turned out to be the father."

Toby shuddered. She couldn't imagine anyone but Jake being the father of her child. She couldn't believe she had ever thought otherwise. It seemed so long ago that she had found out she was pregnant . . . another lifetime . . . a life before Jake. It was a black hole of a life before loving Jake.

Jake closed the door of the study behind him and walked through the dark hall to the front door. He should have phoned the aunts instead of coming to inform them personally of the birth of Adam. They were already making plans. Plans for Adam's future, plans for his and Toby's futures.

He started the Mercedes, a grim smile on his handsome face. The aunts could be gotten around, but the future couldn't. It had to be faced sooner or later, and Jake was afraid that later would be too late. Time was running out for him.

During the months Toby had been with him,

Jake had carefully avoided the matter of her eventual departure. But on the night their son was born she had come to his room to talk to him about leaving. He had been avoiding that memory for two days. It wasn't like him at all to avoid dealing with issues.

He gave a soft laugh. Adam's birth had postponed their talk as effectively as though the son were working with as much determination as the father to keep his parents together.

Jake's smile faded when he thought of how he had tried to explain to the aunts that there was a chance Toby might not be involved in his future. They hadn't seemed to take in what he was saying. He tightened his grip on the steering wheel. How could he expect them to accept her leaving when he couldn't himself?

There had to be a way to keep her with him. At times, late at night, he had been taunted by the temptation to force his will upon her and make her stay. Not physically, but merely by the strength of his arguments. Toby was a strong person, but she didn't know that yet. She could be overcome by logic. He had discovered that when he had convinced her to marry him.

The devil of it was that in coming to love her Jake had lost the ability to force her to bend to his will. And in loving her he had come to need her love as desperately as he needed to give his own. Toby had to stay because she wanted to stay.

He was gripped by a need to start right away showing her that he needed more than friendship, that a loving relationship would be good for them both. But quite frankly he didn't know how to start. Even though she seemed at ease in his company, he remembered how she had acted when she thought he was a threat to her sexually.

There had to be a way to find out what was happening inside Toby's head, some way that wouldn't harm her emotionally. He was afraid of pushing her too far, the way he had on the night before they were married. He needed something to guide him, some kind of clue to what he was dealing with before he began trying to get her to accept him as her husband rather than just the father of her son.

Something had happened to Toby in the past, and it was affecting their present and their future. He had spent long hours thinking about the possibilities, and the conclusions he had come to were not comforting. Rape was an ugly word that he could not force out of his mind no matter how hard he tried. He didn't want to accept the possibility of that kind of horror having been inflicted on his gentle Toby. But he needed to know for sure. If that was the case then he could help her heal. His needs and desires could be shelved indefinitely if she would just let him help her.

But first, he thought with a tight frown, he had to know the truth.

Jake abruptly pulled the Mercedes into a parking lot, circled, then pulled back into traffic in the opposite direction. Dr. Mathias would know. And if he had to force her to tell him what had happened to Toby, then he would.

Pulling up before the small clinic, Jake saw Dr. Mathias walking from the building toward a car parked at the back of the building. He pulled his car up beside her and rolled down the window.

"Dr. Mathias," he said, his grim voice cutting off her greeting. "We need to talk."

She stared thoughtfully, then sighed. "Yes, I guess we do. Would you like to take me to lunch?"

Jake hadn't expected it to be that easy. He glanced at her silently as she slid into the car, then when he felt his shoulder muscles relax he realized how tense he had been.

He didn't attempt to question her until they were seated at a table in a small cafe and the waitress had taken their orders.

"I suppose you know what I want to talk to you about?" he asked cautiously.

She nodded. "Toby." She smiled. "I've watched the progression of your relationship from Toby's perspective since the day she told you about the baby. I guess I expected you to come to me again sooner or later." She regarded him closely. "Does Toby know you're in love with her?"

He caught his breath, closing his eyes, then opened them to stare at her ruefully. "No," he said, his voice strangely raspy. "She doesn't have any idea. She thinks I see her as a friend who just happens to be the mother of my child." He shrugged impatiently. "Do you believe that?"

"Oh yes," she said with a laugh. "There's not much you could tell me about Toby that would surprise me. Now you see what I meant by emotionally immature. She has kept a tight little cocoon around her all her adult life, allowing in only people who don't threaten her security. I was surprised— and a little perturbed—when she allowed you to get close to her because I could see right away that you would threaten the comfortable but false world she had built. Frankly, I was afraid she would wake up too abruptly."

"Why were you afraid? What happened to her?" His intensity was plain in the way he held his body. "I can't try to change things between us, to make it a real marriage, until I know what I'm dealing with. I know she's fragile emotionally and I don't want to harm her, but I can't let her walk out of my life as though there was nothing between us. If I knew what was wrong, I could fix it. I could take care of her."

"I'm afraid it's not something you can fix."

He drew in a deep breath, fixed his eyes on a point across the room, then asked hoarsely, "Rape?"

"No," she said slowly, and he exhaled in harsh relief. But it seemed his relief was premature.

"It wasn't rape, but you're on the right track. It was sexual and it was traumatic." She shifted in her chair. "She was sexually molested when she was eleven years old."

Jake closed his eyes as the pain jolted through him. Anger would come later. Right now all he could think of was Toby's pain, and he let it consume him as though it were his own. His features tightened into a grim mask as the pieces suddenly began to fall together, and he opened his eyes to look at the woman across from him.

"The man she calls Uncle Paul?" he asked stiffly.

She nodded. "I could tell you that he was a sick man and that he loved Toby in his own way, but I have a feeling that wouldn't make any difference to you right now."

"You're right." It was hard to get the words out, and they hurt his throat, coming out in a harsh growl. "It wouldn't make a damn bit of difference. I only wish the son of a bitch was still alive so I could kill him." His fingers turned white, so tightly were his fists clenched. "It wouldn't be an easy death," he rasped out, his eyes on a vision only he could see. "He would regret what he did before—"

"Jake!" Dr. Mathias exclaimed, covering his hands with her own. "You can't let it eat at you. He's gone . . . but Toby's here, and your anger won't help her."

He ran a shaky hand across his tense face.

"You're right. I . . . I can't think right now. Dr. Mathias, what will help her?" He spat out a vicious expletive. "She loved him and he turned her love into something ugly. How could she ever get over that kind of thing? It would have been bad enough if it had been a stranger, but this was a man she loved, the only person in her life who gave her any affection."

"And that's the biggest part of the problem. She blames herself."

"She *what?*" he exploded. "She was a child . . . and he—" He broke off. He couldn't continue the thought without shouting. When he began to speak again, he willed a calmness he didn't feel into his voice. "How could she blame herself?"

"She thinks that because she was so desperate for love she gave him the idea she wanted his advances."

"That's crazy. She was eleven years old."

"You know that and I know that, but Toby doesn't. It's not an uncommon reaction, Jake, but the effects are not usually as drastic as they have been with Toby. Her isolated childhood, the lack of warmth from her parents—all that went into making her what she is today."

She gave him an encouraging smile. "Don't think I'm saying this just to console you, but Toby has taken more steps toward emotional maturity since she met you than I frankly considered possible in such a short span of time. I think she's ready to face what happened to her and accept it. She doesn't have to understand it, just accept that it did happen and that it wasn't her fault."

"How can I help?" He paused. "I'm afraid of wanting too much from her. Is having an intimate relationship with a man too much to expect from her?" He shook his head in frustration. "No, I put that wrong. I don't want her to have a relationship with a man. I want her to have a relationship with me! Is being with me the best thing for Toby?"

"That's something only you and Toby can decide," she said, shrugging. "I can tell you that at least she can handle the question now, even if the answer is the wrong one for you." She inclined her head and smiled. "You've lived with her long enough to know not to startle her with your needs . . . and I think you care for her enough to consider her needs first. Let that be your guide."

Not much of a guide, he thought later as he walked into the hospital. He had driven around after his talk with the doctor, feeling unable to go straight to Toby. First he had to clear up his turbulent thoughts.

He was determined to make up to her for the pain and anguish she had had to deal with in her childhood. He would court her gently, as she deserved to be courted. He would try to make her see him in a new light . . . as a man—a lover— instead of just a friend.

He slowly pushed open the door of Toby's room, wondering how in hell he was going to face her, how he possibly could pretend that things were the same as they were before he had spoken to Dr. Mathias. But he had forgotten the effect Toby always had on him.

When she looked up and saw him standing just inside the door, Toby smiled. It was a soft, slow smile, a smile that made his stomach turn over, that made his muscles dissolve into pure mush. Toby's smile revealed her joy in his mere presence . . . and he almost trembled.

"Jake," she said, extending her hands.

In his rush to grasp her hands, Jake almost tripped over someone sitting beside her bed. He frowned at the intruder, annoyed that he had to share Toby with anyone and annoyed because he was letting the intensity of his feelings for her make him act like a bumbling fool.

"Jake, you remember Lynda," Toby said, smiling shyly.

"Of course he doesn't," the blond woman said as she hastily rose to her feet.

"No, you're wrong," Jake said, relaxing when he saw how nervous Toby's friend was. "You were Toby's maid of honor and you work at SGC. Billing, isn't it?"

Her eyes widened in surprise. "Yes, I do. Imagine you knowing that." She looked from Jake to Toby, then cleared her throat. "I guess I'd better go now, Toby. It was nice seeing you again, Mr. Hammond." She smiled skittishly, moving sideways to avoid him before hurrying out the door.

Jake turned to glance at Toby with raised brows. "What's with her?" he asked. "Have you been telling her that I beat you?"

"And make her jealous?" Toby laughed. "Lynda is not usually shy, but she can't get over the fact that you practically run SGC."

"I don't run it," he denied with a smile. "I work there just like she does." He sat down beside her bed, laying the packages he had been carrying on the floor. "Maybe we should have her over to dinner one night so that she can see that I'm just an ordinary henpecked husband."

"You're not ordinary," she objected. "You're wonderful and"—she gave him a teasing smile—"you are now a father." She leaned her head back and sighed happily. "Have you seen him today?"

"Where do you think I spent the last thirty minutes?" he asked with a rueful laugh, then glanced at her quizzically. "Aren't you even going to ask about the packages?"

"I didn't want to be rude," she said haughtily, then grinned. "Even though I'm dying of curiosity. What's in them?"

Reaching into a bag, he said, "Voila!" as he pulled out a small bouquet of violets.

"Jake," she whispered. "They're beautiful, but why?" She waved her hand toward the flowers decorating every available space in the room. "You've already made the place look like the Botanical Garden."

"Those were for the mother of my son." He picked up her hand and stared down at her slender fingers, then murmured, "These are for you."

Her fingers tightened on his, and when he felt a lump of emotion rise in his throat, he drew in a deep breath and reached into the sack again. "This," he said, smiling, "is for my friend, Toby." He pulled out a small plastic bear and wound it, then sat it on the nightstand so she could watch it march and beat a little plastic drum.

"You're crazy." She laughed as the bear walked off the stand and into her hand.

"And this," he said, reaching into the bag for the third time. "This is for my . . ." He had to force himself to swallow the word "love." Instead he said quietly, ". . . wife."

He handed her the blue leather case and watched her face intently as she opened it.

Toby gasped in surprise when she saw the blue enamel heart on a slender gold chain. "Jake, it's . . . it's the most beautiful thing I've ever seen. Thank you."

When she slid upright in the bed and leaned toward him, Jake caught his breath in surprise, then without thinking, moved toward her irresistibly. Their lips met in a kiss that began spreading a slow warmth through his limbs, then the warmth grew until it blazed throughout his body, tightening his muscles, bringing an ache to his loins.

When he felt ready to grab her and hold her to him roughly, he pulled away and said huskily, "You're beautiful."

She leaned back and gave a breathless laugh. "Lyell said I should be reclining in purple splendor since I've just given birth to the new king."

"Lyell? Your friend from the park?" he asked, keeping the jealousy out of his voice.

She smiled and nodded.

"When was he here?"

"About an hour ago." Toby began to rewind the plastic bear, then glanced up. "I wish he had stayed so you could meet him."

Standing, Jake walked to the other side of the room, then turned, his eyes narrowing as he said stiffly, "Just what is this Lyell like? You seem awfully fond of him."

"I am." She sounded puzzled as though something in his tone disturbed her. "He's very distinguished," she continued slowly. "Handsome in a regal way with loads of old world charm. And he's about sixty."

Jake tried to keep his relief from showing as he gave her a brilliant smile. "Sounds like a wonderful man." He walked back to the bed to sit on the edge. "We'll have to have him over for dinner too." He paused. "I want to get to know all your friends."

Suddenly Toby started to giggle, and the sound held him still. He loved to hear her laugh.

"We should get him together with the aunts," she said, laughing as though she were envisioning the proposed meeting. "It's too bad they never leave their house. Lyell and the aunts getting together might be an event to remember."

"Speaking of the aunts," Jake said, recalling his recent visit. "They have requested that we present Adam to them as soon as possible."

"Adam's first trip out will be one for *him* to remember," she murmured. "I wish we could go now."

He reached down to brush the hair from her forehead. "Tired of hospital food already? How are you feeling?"

"Impatient." Her voice betrayed her frustration. "I want to go home . . . *now.* I want to take Adam home. But when I tell them I'm ready, they all smile like I'm a little backward and poke me to see if I'm done."

He laughed at her belligerent expression.

"It's like none of them were ever mothers," she said mournfully. "If they were, they would know how I feel. They seem totally removed from the real world."

"I'll bet," he said, his voice soothing, "that seventy-five percent of them are mothers. They're just trying to do their jobs."

"Maybe," she said doubtfully. "But not Nurse Jensen," she added, shaking her head forcefully.

He laughed. "Who's Nurse Jensen?"

"She's the one who looks like Ernest Borgnine, and you can't tell me that woman has ever been a mother. A Marine sergeant maybe, but not a mother."

He gave a stifled shout of laughter and leaned over to hug her. "All right, maybe not Nurse Jensen, but even Nurse Jensen can't stop you from coming home when you're ready."

"She could try," Toby whispered, glancing around the room suspiciously, as though the nurse in question had the room bugged. "I wouldn't be surprised if—"

"It's feeding time."

The bright, cheerful voice jerked them both upright. Jake stood and turned around to see a nurse standing at the end of the bed, holding his son casually in one arm. He coughed to disguise his laugh as he recognized the nurse Toby had been telling him about.

She moved with remarkable efficiency, not wasting a moment as she installed Adam in his mother's arms, then she checked her watch and briskly left the room.

Jake turned back to the sound of his son's angry cries. "He sounds ready for an overthrow of the government," he said, watching Adam's red face.

"He's starving to death," Toby murmured as she lowered her gown. "Aren't you, my little anarchist?"

Jake stood hesitantly for a moment, then said slowly, "May I stay, Toby?"

She looked up in surprise. "Of course you can stay. I'm nervous when the nurses are around, but not with you. You're his father, silly."

Jake carefully resumed his place beside her on the bed and gazed down in wide-eyed wonder as his son latched fiercely onto the offered nipple, beating against Toby's breast with a clenched fist.

As he watched, Jake felt emotions welling up inside him that overwhelmed him with their intensity. This was an intimacy that was beyond his experience, and it engulfed him with its sweetness. He felt as though this small woman had given him a priceless gift. A gift that he had to hold on to if his life was to have any meaning at all.

Nine

In the next few weeks the tentative beginning Jake and Toby had made in her hospital room blossomed with the early summer until it had grown into an overpowering awareness of one for the other. Without the other's knowledge, each was anxious to establish new, closer ties in their marriage. But on the other hand each was afraid of pushing ahead too quickly and destroying something fragile and beautiful.

It seemed to Toby that they touched all the time now. Or perhaps it was simply that each touch meant so much to her that it lingered with her to stretch to the next touch and seem a constant in her emotions. And along with the frequency of their caresses came a deepening of the kisses that had before been so casual. She looked forward eagerly to his arrival home each evening because it was an excuse for her to offer him her lips.

In fact, any occasion was an excuse for her to

offer him her lips. When she met him at the breakfast table, many times the food was cold before she slid off his lap, flushed with new and wonderful emotions. Then after rushing through breakfast she walked with him to the door to capture the dizzying sensations again.

Toby smiled now as she stared out at the vivid green outside the glass wall of the den. Their goodbye kiss was taking longer and longer each morning. More often than not, Jake tore his lips from hers with a harried glance at his watch to see that he was late for work. However, his tardiness never seemed to stop him from coming back for a quick encore each time.

And the evenings. . . . The evenings before they separated for the night were spent on the couch, listening to music or reading or perhaps watching television, but always touching, coming together frequently for kisses that grew in intensity with each embrace.

Toby spent her days in a dreamy haze waiting for Jake to come home. The only thing that could force her thoughts to detour from Jake was Adam. But even her beloved son didn't take her away completely. He was included in the feelings that were growing ever stronger inside her. Her son was a part of the love Toby felt for Jake.

Luckily Adam had calmed down somewhat since they had brought him home. But Toby had a definite suspicion it was because the household ran around his schedule. He habitually wore a look of smug contentment, as though he knew he had tamed his environment and had three adults to fulfill his every wish.

"Mrs. Toby?"

Toby turned away from the scene outdoors to find Mrs. Pratt standing beside her.

"Dinner is all prepared. All you have to do is heat and serve." The older woman hesitated. "Are you sure you won't need me tonight?"

"Of course we need you," Toby said, smiling. "But your cousin Phoebe needs you more, so you go on now. And don't worry. We'll be just fine."

She held her dignified pose until Mrs. Pratt walked out the front door, then she almost whooped in excitement. This would be her and Jake's first real evening alone. Adam had been fed and bathed and was sleeping peacefully; Mrs. Pratt was spending the night at her cousin's house; and there had been a look of anticipation in Jake's eyes when he left for work that morning . . . almost as though he were looking forward to the evening as much as Toby was.

She flew around making feverish preparations. She had chosen the table on the patio for their dinner and hurried to lay out the white linen tablecloth, the best silver, and one elegant candle for the center of the table.

Flowers weren't needed. They had a whole garden of flowers surrounding them, and as evening fell the patio became infused with the heady mingled scent of the blossoms.

Toby had spent the better part of the morning choosing what to wear, and now her fingers trembled as she slid into the slim, sea green dress, adjusting the slender straps on her shoulders.

After carefully applying her makeup, she brushed her now shoulder-length hair until it shone, then backed up to view herself in the full-length mirror.

"Well," she said to herself. "It's still Toby, but who cares?" She leaned close to thump the face in the mirror companionably. "You'll do," she said happily. "By golly, you'll do." Then she left her bedroom singing "I Feel Pretty" at the top of her lungs.

She stopped suddenly on her way to the kitchen as the doorbell rang. A timid peek out the window revealed that Lynda was standing at the front door.

"Lynda!" she gasped as she opened the door and pulled her blond friend into the room. "What are you doing here? I mean right now, for heaven's sake?"

"Is it inconvenient?" Lynda asked, looking around the entry hall nervously. "*He's* not home yet is he?"

Toby laughed. "No, *he's* still at work. But even if Jake were home, you would still be welcome." She grinned ruefully. "I didn't sound very welcoming, did I?" Toby gave her friend a quick hug. "I'm a little flustered today. Come on into the den."

Lynda stared at her curiously as they walked into the large room, then as she sat down she said, "Toby, you've changed so much that sometimes I can't believe it."

"For good or bad?" Toby asked, chuckling.

"Definitely for the good." Lynda bit her lip. "And I guess that's why I came to see you. It was a spur of the moment thing." She smoothed down her linen skirt, then glanced up at Toby. "We've been friends for such a long time, Toby. Remember how when we were kids we promised that we would always be friends and if we could ever help each other, we would?"

"Of course I do," Toby said, her voice puzzled. "Do you need help?"

"No, you do."

"Me?" she asked in bewilderment.

"Yes." Lynda sighed and stared down at her hands for a moment. "I talked to my mother today. She's so . . . so happy." Her friend shrugged as though she couldn't find the right words, then reached over to clasp Toby's hand. "Toby, if you hadn't lent her the money to start her dress shop, I don't know what would have happened to her after Daddy died. Sometimes . . . sometimes I think she might have killed herself."

"Lynda!" Toby exclaimed, shocked at what her friend was saying. "You're blowing it out of proportion. Your mother would have been fine. And I didn't do anything. Money is just stuff you put in the bank. You make it sound as though I saved her life. And although I appreciate your gratitude, I think you're making too much out of it."

"No, I'm not," Lynda said, shaking her head vehemently. "When I really needed help, you were there for me. That's what's important."

Toby shifted uncomfortably, then glanced up at Lynda to try again to explain. "Lynda," she said soberly. "When you've got money . . . lots of money . . . it doesn't mean anything to give some of it away. If I had done a worthwhile service for your mother—if I had found her a new husband or something like that—then that would have been real and substantial. But money is nothing. I didn't miss it, and it called for no effort on my part to give it to her."

"It was nothing to you," Lynda said quietly. "But it was everything to Mother. And you didn't hesitate to offer your help because you're my friend." She paused. "That's real and that's substantial."

"Okay," Toby said with a sigh. "If you insist I did something wonderful, I'll take your word for it, but I really don't see why you're bringing it up now. Your mother has already paid the money back, even though I didn't want her to."

"Yes, she's very pleased about that," Lynda said softly. "When I talked to her today, she said that since she has finished paying back your loan she can start expanding." The blond woman stood restlessly and walked to the glass wall to stare outside. "Toby, when she started talking about how grateful she was to you, it made me very ashamed." She whirled around suddenly. "I've never done anything to repay you myself . . . and the favor was for me," she said fervently.

Toby was nonplussed. She didn't know what to say to Lynda. "You've repaid me by just being my friend," she said helplessly.

"No." Lynda shook her head vehemently. "That's not enough. I've been a very casual friend." When Toby started to object, Lynda interrupted. "I have! You know I have!"

As Lynda walked back to the couch, there was a fervent light shining in her eyes that made Toby uneasy.

"I want to help you, Toby," Lynda said eagerly. "The way you helped me. I want to do something important."

Toby stared in wary fascination, then said slowly, "You could lend me five dollars or your new silk dress." When she saw the hurt look on her friend's face, Toby was ashamed of herself for making light of Lynda's offer. "I'm sorry, Lynda." She reached out to squeeze her friend's hand. "I simply don't know what you want from me."

"That's just the point!" Lynda said in exasperation. "I don't want you to do anything. I want to do something for you."

"But I don't need anything," Toby said, laughing at her friend's frustration. "I've got everything I need."

Lynda was silent for a moment, then she said slowly, "How long are you going to stay here, Toby?

And when are you going to tell Jake how much you love him?"

Toby began to shake her head slowly, then gradually the movement became more vigorous. "No, Lynda," she said emphatically. "I don't know what you're thinking, but you can't give me Jake. It doesn't work that way." She smiled sadly. "I'll stay as long as he wants me to, then I'll leave. That's all there is to it."

"Toby, do you even know how he feels about you? Have you ever tried to find out?" She leaned forward, her voice quietly earnest. "Have you talked to his aunts about this? Wouldn't they have some influence with him?"

Toby froze. "You want me to get Miss Sophie and Miss Annabelle to convince him to let me stay?" she whispered incredulously. "I don't want *anyone* to convince him of *anything.*"

"But there are so many people who could talk to him for you," Lynda said, gesturing enthusiastically. "Dr. Mathias or Janine. They could show him how good he is for you. That it would harm you to leave."

Toby sighed, resting her head on the back of the couch, then she said slowly, "Lynda, listen to me. I don't want Jake to feel sorry for me. If I stay it will be because he loves me and for no other reason! That's the way it has to be."

Lynda started to protest again, then she seemed to change her mind. A strange look sparkled in her eyes that caused Toby some concern, but as they settled down to discuss Adam it disappeared, and Toby began to think she had imagined it. By the time Lynda left twenty minutes later, Toby was convinced that she had thoroughly squelched any idea her friend might have about "helping."

Toby stood for a moment in the entry hall, thinking wryly how complicated relationships could be. One simply never knew what was going on in another person's mind.

Then suddenly she realized Jake would be home any minute, and her heart began to pound again, the excitement building inside her to give her face a feverish look.

"Talk about complicated relationships," she muttered on her way to the kitchen.

She was transferring the salad to two small bowls when she heard Jake's car in the drive and she nervously dropped the utensils. She paused to pick up a handful of lettuce from the floor, rinse her hands, and then run at a very unladylike gait to the front door. She slid to a halt and tried to catch her breath, but she was still panting when Jake walked in the door.

She couldn't tell if he noticed anything amiss. He stopped suddenly, staring down at her silently. His face was strangely flushed as he shook his head and said huskily, "Did . . ." He stopped and cleared his throat. "Did Mrs. Pratt get off all right?"

Toby nodded her head, unable to speak as she stared back at him.

"Good." He ran one hand down the side of his slacks, then seemed to notice the bottle in his other hand. "Champagne," he murmured, then closed his eyes briefly and said more firmly, "I bought it for dinner."

"That's wonderful, Jake," she said softly, her eyes widening when it occurred to her at last that—incredibly—Jake was as nervous as she was. "Dinner's almost ready to serve."

"Good," he said again. He opened his mouth, as though he wanted to add something else, then shook his head and said lamely, "Fine."

He mumbled something else under his breath,

then began to loosen his tie, his movements jerky. "I think I'll take a shower, Toby." As he turned away she heard his muttered, "Maybe it'll clear away the cobwebs in my brain."

He sounded totally disgusted with himself. She gave a short laugh as she put the champagne on ice and put things onto a tray to carry to the patio.

When she had arranged everything just so, she went in search of Jake and met him just as he was coming out of his room, his hair still damp from the shower. He had dressed in a fresh suit and tie. She stared at his strong face for a moment, but for some reason her stare seemed to make him more nervous, so she glanced away.

"It's all ready," she said brightly. "I thought we would eat on the patio. It seems more rom . . . nicer."

"That's great," he said, then expelled a huge gust of air in exasperation. Grabbing her hand, he muttered, "Come on, for heaven's sake. Let's eat."

Later as she watched the candlelight play across the strong lines of his face, she thought how odd it was that they had both decided tonight would be special. Neither of them ate more than a token amount of food, and conversation was impossible. Toby was too full of his presence, too aware of the electric tension that surrounded them to speak of trivial things.

Every time she lifted her fork to her lips, she would glance up to see him watching her with a deep, disturbing intensity and she would become lost in the blue of his eyes. They would stare for countless moments in silence, then one or the other of them would realize what was happening and break the spell. They would each move the food about on their plates or use their napkins to wipe their lips, until the whole thing began again the next time their eyes met.

At last they silently agreed that the meal was officially over and together they moved to the den. Jake turned down the lights and put a record on the stereo while Toby smoothed her dress, then her hair, turning this way and that as she tried to relax. The music wasn't helping any. It filled the room with a throbbing intensity. She hadn't known that classical music could be so sensual.

When he sat beside her on the couch, he drew in a raspy breath and turned to her, his chin jutting out with determination. "Do you feel as ridiculous as I do?" he asked dryly.

She giggled and shook her head up and down vigorously. "What's wrong with us?"

"I think we're trying to force things to happen when they should be evolving naturally." He picked up her hand. "Toby, I would like very much to kiss you. Do you suppose we could handle that without making a mess of it?"

"We . . ." She cleared her throat and continued in a whisper. "We can only do our best."

Her head dropped to the back of the couch and her eyelids drooped as he moved closer. She kept her eyes on his firm mouth, taking in the sensual fullness of his lower lip, aching to feel it against hers. Then her eyes closed at his first tentative touch. In the past two months they had kissed often and with much pleasure, but it was as though they both knew that this time was different.

She felt every nerve ending in her lips come vibrantly alive as he moved his mouth on hers. She sighed as his tongue caressed her lower lip, and he took the opportunity to deepen the kiss, moving his tongue slowly into the recesses of her mouth until she was swamped by the drugging desire his kiss brought.

She raised her hands to his shoulders and touched the muscles there, hard and under strict control, as though he were afraid to let himself relax. She moved her hand under his collar to massage his warm, strong neck, then gasped when her movement brought a deep, painful-sounding groan from him.

He moved suddenly, and before she realized what was happening she was lying beneath him on the couch and his face was buried in her throat as he murmured hoarsely against her flesh, the heat of his breath surprising her.

"Toby," he whispered with ragged hunger. "My God, Toby."

She had never seen Jake out of control before. It didn't frighten her; instead the thought brought incredible pleasure, and she raised her hands to clasp his head, holding him close. She moved her body against his in a spontaneous reaction to his lovemaking, feeling desire rise up in her. It was as though her actions were taken out of her control, too . . . as though her body knew the secret goal of which her mind was ignorant.

Her shoulders were caught in a rough grasp, and as he kissed her throat and the rounded flesh of her breasts, he slid his hand beneath the strap of her dress. He urgently began pushing the strap aside. Then suddenly, as it broke beneath his feverish caress, Jake raised up. His face had a stunned expression as he stared down at her. He took in her disheveled hair, the torn strap, and a sound of anguish broke from his throat.

He shoved himself off the couch and stood for a moment beside her. Turning slowly, he reached back to her, then slammed his hand against his leg and walked out of the room.

Toby lay where he had left her, unable to comprehend the exact meaning of the events that had just taken place. But soon she forgot about what had happened between them on the couch and concentrated instead on the expression she had seen on Jake's face as he had left the room. She didn't know what had caused that look of pain, but she knew she couldn't just let it go. She couldn't stand the thought of him being unhappy.

Rising slowly, she moved down the hall and quietly pushed open the door to his bedroom. He hadn't turned on the light, but she could see him sitting on the edge of his bed. He had discarded his jacket, his shirt was open at the throat, and his hands were resting on his knees as he bent forward.

Walking soundlessly across the thick carpet, she stopped beside him and reached out to touch his hair. "Jake?"

He jerked his head up, then when he saw her standing there, he grasped her hand, closing his eyes as he brought it to his lips to press a feverish kiss to the soft palm. After a tense moment, he groaned and let it fall back to her side and stood to pace before her.

"I'm sorry, sweetheart," he whispered urgently. "I'm so damn sorry." He ran his hand through his hair. "I know it's no excuse, but I've been going crazy . . . trying to live like a damned eunuch . . . and all the time you're there in the next room. So lovely . . . so damned lovely."

He swiveled sharply and walked to the window. "I lost my head. I'm sorry, but that's what happened. You touched me and I lost my stupid head." He slammed a fist into his palm. "I've been so careful about keeping myself under control. And it was working." He leaned his head against the wall wearily. "Dammit to hell, it was working and I blew it."

Toby stood beside the bed and stared at him in stunned surprise. She had never seen him so angry. It was as though the last piece of the puzzle had fallen into place. Now she knew Jake—knew him and loved him more than she ever thought possible.

Walking across the room, she stopped directly in front of him. "Jake," she said quietly. "I wanted you to be passionate with me. I've wanted it for a long time now."

She could almost feel all his muscles tighten, and his features appeared frozen in the soft moonlight. She gave a nervous laugh. "Should I not have said it straight out like that? Am I being too forward?"

He ran a hand across his face, then gave her a stunned look. "No . . ." he whispered hoarsely, then he drew in a deep breath. *"God, no."*

"After Adam was born," she continued softly, "I began to wonder about the night we'd spent together. I was feeling things for you that I'd never felt before, and I wondered just how much that medication had to do with that night." She inhaled slowly. "So I called Dr. Mathias and asked her. She said . . . she said it wouldn't have changed my personality." Toby stared down at her hands. "Which means that I made love to you that night because I wanted to."

She felt him move beside her, but she wanted to finish before he touched her again. "I felt odd at first. You have to remember it was my first experience with . . . desire. I expected to feel sick or at least ashamed." She looked up and the look on his face caused a painful joy to pierce her heart. "But I didn't," she whispered huskily. "I was glad . . . because it was you."

Before the last word left her lips she was in his arms, and their lips met in a fiery kiss. She ran her hands over his chest, reveling in the feel of him. And when she sensed that there was still some hesitancy in his movements, she took a step away from him.

"Jake," she said in a pleading whisper. "There is not a single thing you could do to me that would frighten me." Then she reached behind her to slide the zipper of her dress down her back.

He caught his breath, then pulled her back into his arms. "You darling," he moaned against her lips. "You beautiful, wonderful darling."

After that there was no more hesitation. The hunger that had been building in them both forced urgency into their actions as they hurriedly undressed each other and fell together onto the bed. Toby felt the desperate need in his body, saw it in his harshly drawn features, and it moved her to tears. Even if she hadn't wanted him just as badly, she could never ignore that need. It made her want to give all that was in her to give and hope that it was enough.

And when she felt his naked body sliding against hers, she stopped thinking altogether. His hands touched her with a primitive desire that echoed her own, his rough palms spreading across her body, tracing every inch of flesh, which was his for the taking. Each touch she received, each touch she gave was a revelation to her uninitiated mind.

"Toby." His hoarse whisper was an added caress on the smooth flesh of her shoulder. "I would have died if you hadn't come to me tonight."

She shivered as the words reached a deep, hidden part of her. Each different sensation—his strong body crushing hers; the hair of his chest roughly caressing her breasts; his tongue moving from her neck to her ears to her mouth, devouring her in an elemental need—melded together into one glorious, earth-shaking experience.

Jake needed her. *Her.* Toby Baxter Hammond was needed. It was like nothing she had ever felt before. His need and her own desire were a highly combustible combination. Emotion surged up inside her, and when he lowered his mouth to her breast she clasped her hands to his head, pressing him into her full flesh, arching her hips beneath him.

They came together with the natural grace of two healthy animals, and Toby no longer had to wonder what she had felt on that night so long ago. It was the most incredibly beautiful thing she had ever experienced. No matter what happened to her in the future, nothing could take away the knowledge that for those precious moments she was one with Jake.

She buried her face in his neck, hearing him cry out her name repeatedly, then suddenly he took her over the edge and led her to fulfillment . . . and she cried.

As he came down from the shuddering high, Jake felt the tears on Toby's face and rolled over so that she lay beside him. He carefully wiped them away with the tips of his fingers, then dipped his head to catch the remaining moisture with his lips. He didn't have to ask her why she was crying. He knew. Deep down in the heart of him he knew what she was feeling—because he felt the same.

It was like the first time they had made love, but then it was different. He couldn't yet straighten out in his mind what had happened to him.

Tonight with Toby he had found something he had been looking for all his life. He had found the other half of himself.

He looked down at her, and if she had opened her eyes at that moment she would have seen the love that he couldn't hide. Such a small woman, he thought in amazement. Such a small woman to hold such a big part of his heart.

He knew now that even if they had not been blessed with a child he still would have fallen in love with Toby. He had been captivated by her from their very first meeting, and the love that had been buried deep inside him had grown forcefully until it could no longer be ignored. Now that they had moved into a new phase in their relationship, he would make being with him difficult for her to give up. Somehow he would make her fall in love with him. He couldn't rest until he knew that the overwhelming love he felt for her was returned. Now more than ever he needed that love.

She moved against him as her breathing gradually returned to normal, then slowly she opened her eyes, and the look there made him want to join her in tears. Wrapping one arm around his neck, she laid her head on his chest, curling her body into his. They lay in silence, no words necessary to express what they had shared.

Toby listened to the even sound of Jake's breathing, then rolled onto her side, propping herself up on her elbow to stare at him as he lay on his back with his eyes closed. She sighed when his eyes remained closed, then after a few seconds, sighed again, this time louder. She saw his lips twitch slightly and knew he was awake.

Reaching out slowly she tickled him under his

chin, then let out a squeal of delight when his hand came out to jerk her on top of him.

"Can't you let a contented man enjoy his contentment in peace?" he growled against her neck.

"No," she said stubbornly. "I'm too happy to be still and quiet. I'm . . . I'm *exploding* with happiness." She began to kiss him all over his face.

He laughed, moving his head to dodge her noisy kisses. "And this is the woman I was afraid would break if I touched her," he said, cupping her buttocks to hold her squirming body still. "I misjudged you badly."

"So did I." She propped her elbows on his chest. "Misjudged myself, I mean. I thought I would fall apart if I ever made love. I honestly thought I would be sick all over the place." She grinned, leaning down to kiss his strong nose. "Aren't you glad I was wrong?"

Sliding from beneath her, he cradled her head on his shoulder, then said slowly, "Why did you think that, Toby?"

For a moment she held herself tense as though she were unable to answer, then exhaling in a long sigh she said quietly, "Because of Uncle Paul. It's a gruesome story, Jake, and believe me you don't want to hear it. Suffice it to say he prejudiced me against men and sex."

He moved to gaze down at her thoughtfully. "I know what happened, Toby. Dr. Mathias told me." He gave her a kiss of apology. "I wanted you to trust me enough to tell me about it yourself."

She glanced away to stare at the wall opposite the bed. "I don't know if I like the idea of you discussing me with someone else . . . not even Dr. Mathias," she said finally. "What did you think about . . . about what she told you?"

Toby didn't look at him for a while, then she felt

the tension building in the muscles she rested against, and she rolled over to grip his neck in an effort to avoid the explosion she sensed was coming.

"Don't Jake," she said, kissing his stiff lips. "You can't let the past rip you up."

She rose slightly to frame his harsh face with her hands. "That's what you've taught me tonight. I missed being a real person for so many years—not because of what Paul tried to do to me, but because of the way I held on to it and let it affect me. It's all gone," she said, her deep gratitude showing in her face. "I'll never be afraid to take a chance on life again. Because even if I fail at least I'm living and trying and growing."

"You've got more charity in your soul than I do," he said fiercely, but she could feel him relaxing beneath her.

"No, you're wrong." Her voice was quiet. "I didn't say I forgave him. I don't think I ever could . . . especially now that we've got Adam and I know how truly vulnerable children are. But I will not allow another human being to manipulate my life. From now on I take control. My actions will not be reactions—to the past, to hurtful incidents. They will be the result of conscious decisions on my part." She gave a laugh, unaware of how free it sounded. "From now on I'm the captain of my own rowboat, and it goes where *I* tell it to."

Jake was silent for so long as he lay with his eyes closed, Toby began to wonder what was going on in his mind. At last he said, "Where will you tell it to go, I wonder?" He opened his eyes, and she was mesmerized by the blaze of blue light. "Steer it in my direction, please, Toby," he whispered urgently, then pulled her head down to his, and the magic began again.

Ten

When morning came to bring the lovers back to earth, it was a wondrous day, a day out of a fairy tale, a day of new beginnings. And Adam would not be excluded from Toby and Jake's beautiful day. He aroused them early, while they were still deep in dreams of the night before.

Toby woke up slowly and felt something tickling her ear. She brushed it away with a lazy hand, then snuggled deeper into the covers. But the tickling began again, and this time when she tried to brush it away, she found her hand caught in a rough grasp. She opened her eyes and saw Jake propped up on one elbow watching her with a strange smile on his face.

"Do you know what I regret about last night?" he asked softly, brushing his hand across her neck and shoulders.

"You regret something?" she asked, her voice still husky with sleep.

"Yes, I do." He laid his head back and pulled closer so that her head lay on his shoulder. "I regret that you weren't wearing that gown you got as a wedding present." He closed his eyes. "You don't know how many times I've envisioned taking that gown off you."

She turned her face and began moving her lips slowly across his chest. "Shall I put it on now . . . so you can take it off?" she whispered.

"Ah, love," he moaned. "The world intrudes. The world in the form of an impatient young man."

He slid his hand down her back to her rounded buttocks, his fingers pressing into the soft flesh to bring her closer for a brief moment.

"Your son, madam," he said with a resigned sigh, "is awake and demanding his breakfast." He laughed softly, leaning down to kiss her on the tip of her nose. "If he were more my size I would show him who's boss."

"Afraid of him, huh?" she asked as she stretched in lazy contentment. Then when Adam's belligerent cries were heard again, she grinned at the healthy sounds and slid from the bed to make her way to the nursery.

"Okay, okay, you ferocious little monster," she laughed as she pulled his knit sleeper over his head to change his diaper. It was a struggle, but she eventually got Adam into clean clothes, luckily before his indignant demands reached an ear-splitting level.

As she sat in the wooden rocker, Jake moved to stand behind her, bringing his hand up to rest on her warm breast. She lifted one hand to press his closer, then glanced up at him with a happy, contented smile.

" 'Madonna and Child,' " he murmured as he stared down at the two of them.

"Raphael or Modigliani?" she asked dreamily. At that moment Adam came up for air and burped noisily. "Well," she sighed. "It was a nice thought anyway."

"How about 'Madonna and Uncouth Little Twit,' " he suggested wryly, "by Andy Warhol?" He leaned down and kissed her on the nape of the neck. "I'm afraid," he said in a husky whisper, "that our son takes after me, Toby. He's greedy for what only you can give."

Toby watched him leave the room to dress, and she wanted desperately to believe that he meant what he had said. That he needed something only she could give.

Today, she told herself wistfully, for today only, she would pretend it was the truth. Tomorrow she would worry about the future. For this one wonderful day she would pretend it was forever.

And it was a wonderful day, a fabulous day. For Jake, watching as his wife carried his son on her hip, moving about the garden to pick flowers, it was as though he had been reborn, starting life over with the exuberance that should have been there the first time. He hadn't known how dreary his life had become until he met Toby. A pattern had been set years earlier, and he couldn't disentangle himself enough to see how meaningless his existence had become. It took a revolutionary disruption in the form of Toby Baxter Hammond to shake him loose and show him what was missing.

After holding her in his arms all night, after the incredible closeness, he felt a dangerous sense of possession. He was becoming obsessed with her in a way he had never thought possible. He had thought, before they made love, that if he could assuage the consuming physical desires that he felt for her, he would come down from the tremendous high of loving her and his emotions would settle down to an ordinary love. But it wasn't so. If anything his feelings for her were more intense than before. The love he felt for her filled every pore, and he was sure her presence in his mind and body had to be visible to the naked eye.

For Toby the day was a hiatus in her war to win Jake, a lovely day set aside to enjoy what they had found together before taking up the problems still facing them. She gloried in her new-found maturity. It was as though fate had finally accepted her as an adult, letting her in on the marvelous secrets a fulfilled woman is privileged to. She was aware of her body in a way she had never been before. She was aware of the miracle of life itself in a way she had never been before. It amazed her that one night could make all the difference in the way she viewed the world around her. It was as though she had been blind and was suddenly given the gift of sight.

While Toby stood with wide-eyed wonder, gazing at the loveliness of the garden, Jake lay with his son beside him on a blanket beneath a spreading oak. Just as he was about to doze off, he felt Toby's hands moving in his hair, but kept his eyes closed, enjoying the pleasure of her nearness, reveling in the knowledge of their intimacy.

At last without opening his eyes, he said lazily, "Are you weaving a spell, witch?"

"No," she whispered, and her voice was close to his ear. "I'm weaving a crown for a king among men."

He opened one eye and reached up to touch his hair. "Toby," he said, letting the eye drift closed again. "Are there flowers in my hair?"

"Um-hum," she said, moving her lips softly against his neck. "I couldn't find any laurel leaves

. . . so I used purple periwinkles." She paused. "The effect is . . . stunning."

"Adam is too young to lose his mother," he said quietly.

"Is that a threat?"

He raised himself on one elbow to stare down at her as she lay beside him. "No," he said simply as he moved to cover her body. When he felt her softness beneath him his breathing became erratic, and he whispered, "How do you feel about making love to a man with petunias in his hair?"

"Periwinkles," she corrected, moving her hands to his neck. "I would never make love to a man wearing petunias. But periwinkles . . . well, periwinkles are something else. Periwinkles"—she slid her hands down his chest to his waist and pressed down—"turn me on."

"Remind me to stock up on purple periwinkles," he groaned as he lowered his head to cover her impudent mouth with his, and the only sounds in the garden for quite a while were the humming of the bees and the small snorting sounds Adam made occasionally when he slept.

"Jake," Toby said breathlessly as he spread open her shirt to bury his face against her breasts. "Jake, I think I heard the doorbell."

"You couldn't have." He moved the fabric of her blouse aside to test new ground. "No one would be inconsiderate enough to bother us on a day like today."

But even as he spoke they heard the sound again, and he exhaled a harsh breath as he left her arms to stand up. Picking up the still sleeping Adam, Toby handed him to Jake, then stood up to follow.

As they walked she began to laugh, and when he glanced at her inquisitively, wanting to share her amusement, she gasped, "Jake, you would probably do something deadly to me if I let you answer the door, wouldn't you?"

"I don't mind answering the door," he said in bewilderment.

"With flowers in your hair?"

"Damn, I forgot," he said with a wry smile. "Get them out."

"What'll ya give me?" she asked moving away from him. His hands were full of Adam, and she stood back regarding the purple flowers that were twined in his hair.

When he moved toward her menacingly, she raised a hand and laughed. "Okay, you win. Bend your head down." She began to pull the flowers from his hair with a silent, "He loves me. He loves me not."

By the time they got to the den only one flower remained, and she closed her eyes in happiness as she murmured a relieved, "He loves me," under her breath.

She let Jake go on to the front door while she lay Adam down in his crib. As she stood in the dim light of the nursery looking down at her son, she thought of the night before and the incredible closeness she and Jake had found. The night had not contained much sleep for either of them. When they were not touching, learning each other's bodies, they were talking, learning each other's minds.

But even with the intimacies that had passed between them, Toby knew that she couldn't let it rest. Tomorrow she would have to begin her campaign again and keep working at it until Jake felt the way she did. The lovemaking they had experienced the night before had been wonderful, but Toby still wanted more. She wanted a love that would last forever. She wanted to be with Jake when they were too old to make love. The thought of spending the rest of her life without him terrified her, and she prayed she would have the strength to live by his decision when the time came.

Giving her son one last pat, she walked back into the den, then stopped suddenly when she saw Lyell and Lynda looking extremely uncomfortable as they stood beside Jake.

"Lyell. Lynda," she said in surprise. "How nice of you to . . . drop by," she finished in a gulp, then when she saw the fearful look on Lynda's face, her eyes narrowed and she said, "Lynda, you didn't—"

"We're sorry to intrude," Lyell said regally, "but Lynda came to the park today, and we began to discuss our mutual friend—yourself, Toby. It became clear very soon in the conversation that neither of us would feel entirely comfortable until we at least tried to do something about your ridiculous situation, my dear."

"My ridiculous . . . But what—" she began, turning to stare in confusion at Jake, who merely shrugged and shook his head at her questioning look.

"We're here because we're your friends, Toby," Lynda said defensively. "Because you won't help yourself."

"Lynda," Toby said, shaking her head weakly. "Oh Lynda." She sighed. "Sit down, both of you." Toby moved closer to Jake, trying to form some kind of explanation, but since she didn't understand what was happening herself she couldn't very well explain to him.

"Toby."

She glanced at Lyell as he began to speak.

"I've been thinking about what you told me in

the hospital, young Toby," Lyell said. "And after speaking to Lynda I came to the conclusion—"

"Wait," Toby interrupted. "I know what Lynda thinks and she's wrong. Lyell, listen to me—" But before she could try to reason with him the doorbell rang again.

"I'll get it, Toby," Jake said, amusement and curiosity spreading across his features as he left her alone with her friends.

"Lynda, why did you do this?" Toby asked urgently as soon as Jake left the room. "I thought we decided yesterday—" Before she could go any further Toby heard voices in the hall, and her eyes widened in stunned amazement when Dr. Mathias and Janine walked into the den.

"Toby," Janine said, moving across the room to clasp Toby's hands. "Lynda has told me a little of your situation, and after talking to Dr. Mathias I felt that I should come . . . since you've stopped seeing me regularly. I really feel that we need to talk about this."

Dr. Mathias gave Toby an apologetic glance. "I'm sorry, Toby. I tried to stop her. Please remember that above all else we care about you."

"Yes," she murmured, "yes, of course." Then she shook her head and raised her voice impatiently. "Now will someone please tell me what's going on?"

They all began to talk at once, and she could make no sense whatever out of what was said. She gathered they were trying to help in some way, but no one would tell her just what it was they were trying to accomplish.

"Please," she said, her voice taking on a harried quality. "Please, everyone sit down and tell me—one at a time," she added warily, "just what it is you want me to do. If we discuss this calmly, I'm sure—"

"Toby!" Jake called from the hall.

Toby shrugged helplessly and moved out of the den, relieved to be away from the room that seemed to be growing inexplicably crowded. She walked up to Jake and put her arms around his waist to look up at him. "What are they all doing here?" she whispered urgently.

"I don't know," he muttered, "but look."

She moved to stand in front of him and looked out the window as he held the drapes open. Coming up the front drive was the most fantastic car she had seen in her life. It was long and square and had thin, wire wheels. The driver's seat was out in the open, and the rest of the car was closed. Toby looked for a fleur de lis, but someone had evidently forgotten to put it on. However nothing else in the way of trappings had been left off. It gleamed green and black and chrome.

"What is it?" she whispered in shock.

"It's a 1918 Isotta Fraschini."

"A *what?*"

"An Isotta Fraschini. Rudolph Valentino had one just like it," Jake said, unable to keep the laughter out of his voice. "And more importantly, it's carrying the aunts."

"But—but," she sputtered. "They never leave their house. You told me so."

"They don't," he confirmed. "But by God, they did." He shook his head. "I don't believe it. I really don't believe it. I talked to them yesterday, and they didn't say a word about coming over."

As the car drew closer, Toby could see that instead of a chauffeur Miss Sophie was driving the car and Miss Annabelle was sitting beside her, vehemently gesturing toward the house as she held onto her hat.

Toby and Jake glanced at each other in resignation, then walked outside to usher the elderly women inside.

"We're so glad you decided to visit us," Toby said weakly as the two women entered the house. "Would you like to take off your hats and come into the—" She couldn't take them into the den. "—the parlor?"

Miss Sophie cocked her head when she heard voices coming from the back of the house and began to walk in that direction. "This room will be fine for what we came to do," she said over her shoulder as she marched toward the den with Miss Annabelle trailing behind, smiling pleasantly as she murmured, "So nice . . ." in a vague voice.

As they reentered the room, Lyell was saying vigorously, ". . . but it's not right for Toby to put Jake's happiness before hers. It's very noble of her, but why should she neglect her own needs?"

Janine leaned forward before he could continue. "Toby will make her own happiness. She's not dependent on another human being for that."

"Selfish, selfish," Miss Sophie exclaimed, walking into the middle of the melee. "People cannot live selfishly. You're both talking about Toby's happiness—and of course we're all concerned with that—but what about Jacob's? Doesn't he deserve a little happiness?"

"It's Jake's happiness that Toby is concerned about," Lynda interjected. "That's why we're here. Lyell and I were talking—"

"I really think this is something Toby and I should discuss privately," Janine said vehemently.

"Jake said—"

"Toby told me—"

"When Lynda called—"

Toby glanced around the room in confusion. Lynda and Lyell were sitting on the couch arguing with Janine, who was pacing in the middle of the room. Miss Sophie was sitting in Jake's chair, arguing with anyone who would listen. And Miss Annabelle and Dr. Mathias seemed to be having a cozy little chat in the corner of the room.

Suddenly she felt a hand on her arm. She turned as Jake lifted a finger to his lips and gestured toward the door. No one seemed to notice as the two of them left the room.

When they were safely inside his study, Jake closed the door behind them and leaned against it with a sigh of relief. "I said I wanted to get to know your friends," he said wryly, "but I didn't think there would be an invasion. I had something more conventional in mind, like a nice, casual dinner." He laughed in genuine amusement. "Now, do you know what in hell is going on?"

"I don't have the slightest idea," she said weakly. "Lynda came by yesterday and . . . we talked— about her mother and our friendship—but I never expected anything like this. She asked me when I was going to leave, and other than the usual stuff about Adam that was all we discussed."

He stood silently for a moment. "What did you tell her?" At her questioning glance he added, "About leaving. When did you say you would leave?"

His voice was stiff, and she detected a touch of anger in it that surprised her. She shrugged nervously. "I simply told her I would leave it up to you. That I would leave when you wanted me to."

"And that's why she thinks you're throwing away your happiness on me?" He stepped closer, clenching his fists as his voice grew louder. "And did you tell your peculiar friend Lyell the same thing?"

"*My* peculiar friend," she said tightly. "*My*?

What about Arsenic and Old Lace in there. Why are they here? Obviously they think you're sacrificing your happiness for mine." She stepped closer to him, glaring up at him belligerently. "What right do you have to call my friends strange?"

"You were the one who said they were 'adorable,' " he mimicked, bending his head as he raised his voice. "*I've* always known the aunts were strange." He turned and ran his hand through his hair in frustration. "And I don't know why they're here. They also asked me how long you were staying when I talked to them yesterday."

"And what did you tell them?" she asked stiffly.

"I said that was up to you," he said, waving his hand in exasperation.

She moved across to where he stood and jerked on his arm furiously. "So they were right," she shouted in his face. "Who do you think you are? What makes you think I want that kind of sacrifice from you. You—you—"

"Toby," he said in astonishment as he stared down at her angry features. "Toby, you're yelling. You're furious and . . . we're having an honest-to-God argument."

She stared at him as though he were mad, then suddenly her eyes widened in surprise and she grinned. "We are, aren't we? I don't think I've ever had an argument before. And I know I've never lost my temper." She laughed. "Is it always this much fun?"

"No." He chuckled. "So we won't do it often." His face sobered. "Toby, all this garbage about sacrifices—"

"Yes, I forgot about that," she said, then frowned. "Jake, I'll leave when you want me to. I don't want to stay if it's getting in the way of your life."

"How can—" he exploded, then stopped with a grimace and continued in a gentler voice. "How can you talk about getting in my way after last night?"

She saw the hurt look on his face and leaned against him, rubbing her cheek on his chest. "Last night was beautiful, but how long does that kind of thing last?"

He reached down to turn her face up so he could see her. "Forever, Toby," he whispered, his voice ragged with emotion. "For me it lasts forever. So that just leaves you."

"Oh Jake," she said, framing his face with her hands. "If that means you love me, then me too. I've loved you for such a long time and I was ready to . . . to *burst* with the need to tell you." She leaned her forehead against his chin. "I was afraid you were going to tell me to go."

His arms came around her in a rough hold as he pressed her to him tightly. "That would never happen, sweetheart. Don't you know that if you left you'd be taking the best part of me with you? I've wanted to tell you for months how I felt about you, but I was afraid I would scare you." He inhaled sharply; it was a harsh, painful sound. "I watched every move I made because I was terrified I would do something wrong and you would want to leave."

She made a sound that was a cross between a laugh and a moan. "And I was driving myself crazy trying to find a way to stay." She ran her hands over his back possessively. "Do you want to know what I thought about last night?"

He looked down at her with raised brows, and she gave a short laugh. "Besides that. I thought about that fervent speech I subjected you to when you asked me to marry you. The one about heroes." She paused as she realized in shock how long ago that all seemed. "I still don't know about the spectacular, world famous heroes . . . however I'm willing to give them the benefit of a doubt now," she said magnanimously, then hid her face to add softly, "But since I've come to know you . . . and to love you, I've learned something more important. There are other heroes—everyday heroes, personal heroes who are never recognized. Men like you," she said, reaching up to touch his face, "who do the heroic on a daily basis, not for glory but because that's the way they're made."

"Toby," he whispered huskily, his voice shaking with some strong emotion. "That's too much. I didn't . . . I don't—"

She put a hand to his lips. "No, I know you don't think of yourself that way. And I won't try to convince you." She ran her fingers over the lips that trembled beneath her touch. "But don't try to convince me that you're not . . . because I know the truth."

As he groaned and dipped his head to still her lips, the love between them was at last given free rein, and it took awhile for them to come back to earth. What they'd shared in the study would remain precious to them both for the rest of their lives, but eventually a little sanity crept back into their thoughts, and Jake looked down at her as they sat together in his leather chair.

"Do you have any idea why all those people are in our den?" he said huskily.

She laughed. "I think they're here to save our marriage. Lyell and Lynda both know I love you and that I didn't want to leave."

"And the aunts and Dr. Mathias know how much you mean to me," he said with a laugh. "So we must have been talking in circles during our argument."

"I have a feeling the surprise party was organized by Lynda. She'll be glad to know that although we didn't listen to their arguments their arrival was at least a catalyst." She shook her head. "It doesn't matter," she whispered, leaning against him with a sigh. "I loved our argument, even if it was unnecessary." She took his hand and pushed it inside her blouse. "I plan on having at least one a week."

"Do you really think that's necessary?" he asked warily.

"Sure," she said, smiling in an innocently seductive gesture. "If you doubt it, just remember how you felt when the quarreling was over and we made up."

"You may have a point there," he whispered. Then as their eyes met he lowered his head to cover her lips with his own, and they tried again to feed the hunger that was never fully appeased.

Sometime later Miss Annabelle Hammond left the den and wandered into the hall, searching diligently for the ladies' room. As she reached a door on her right, she opened it quietly, then stood there, her fragile features still in comical amazement as she saw what the room contained.

After gasping a surprised, *"Oh, my,"* she closed the door behind her and walked back toward the den with a smile of pleased excitement on her thin face, calling, "Sister, you'll never guess . . ."

Jake never quite lost the look of wonder that came into his eyes when Toby walked into a room. He had met her when she was still a child, and he watched her grow into lovely womanhood. He encouraged her to do something with her special knack with children and was beside her when she graduated with a degree in physical therapy. He was never afraid that she would grow away from him because he saw her daily growing closer until she became part of him mentally and physically, a part that would have killed the whole if it were removed.

Toby continued to see Jake as the man who took her away from darkness and brought her into the light. She could never do enough to show him her love, even though, true to her word, she saw to it that they had a vigorous argument every now and then. Even when their three children were grown and brought their own children to visit, Toby was teased about her Prince Charming.

But she didn't mind the teasing about fairy tales. She had all she had ever wanted in life, and she knew the truth of the matter. For you see, they *did* live happily ever after.

THE EDITOR'S CORNER

Readers who are new to our LOVESWEPT romances have been writing to ask how they can get copies of books we published during our first year on sale. So I thought it might be helpful for me to point out that a list of our books, accompanied by an order form, can be found in the backs of many of our LOVESWEPT romances. (Once in a while there isn't enough space for the whole list—due to my Editor's Corner being too long!) If you send the form along with your check to the address indicated on the blank, our folks in Des Plaines will get your order back to you within four to six weeks. In future LOVESWEPT books, you'll be seeing all or a part of a listing that we put together. It gives just a few lines of description about each of our first fifty titles; if you've missed any of them, do be sure to order.

Speaking of being missed . . . doesn't two months seem too long to wait for another of Helen Mittermeyer's powerful love stories? Next month you'll be treated to **VORTEX,** LOVESWEPT #67, by Helen, and it's just the sort of dramatic romance you've come to expect from this talented storyteller. Heroine Reesa Hawke is beautiful, spirited . . . and troubled; Dake Masters is as magnetic and forceful and attractive as a hero can be. Reesa and Dake have been separated for seven long months, months in which Reesa remembered nothing about her life before a fisherman pulled her out of the storm-tossed waters of the Caribbean Sea. When Dake suddenly appears, bringing back the torrid memories of their life together, Reesa finds herself just as wildly attracted as in the past, but with a wealth of new and enriching insights into the values that had

(continued)

been missing in their relationship. Yet Dake is a changed person, too. How they reconcile their troubled past and their optimism for the future makes for a provocative and tender love story that you won't want to miss.

Another very talented Helen—Helen Conrad—provides a delightful romp in **UNDERCOVER AFFAIR,** LOVESWEPT #68. Helen's heroine Shelley Pride and hero Michael Harper certainly meet in a unique way: Shelley captures him . . . literally . . . in a citizen's arrest! But soon Michael turns the tables, hotly pursuing the woman he's discovered he can't live without. A merry chase follows and reserved Shelley is forced to unbend—even, at one point, to become a daring impostor! There's danger, too, though, because of Michael's work, and the lovers are almost parted by it. I'll bet that you're going to relish the way Michael "shadows" Shelley . . . as well as all the other heartwarming episodes in **UNDERCOVER AFFAIR.**

It's always exciting for us to bring you new talent—and never more so than next month when Marianne Shock debuts as a published author with **QUEEN'S DEFENSE,** LOVESWEPT #69. Witty, warm, and just plain wonderful, this romance gets off to a marvelous start when heroine China Payne's mother—she's just a little batty—threatens to hire a "hit man" to go after her fifth husband. That gentleman happens to be hero Reeve Laughlin's father. What follows between China and Reeve is a love affair to remember . . . coupled with a chess game that predicts the bold moves of a well-matched man and woman. I believe you'll be delighted to join us in giving a warm welcome to Marianne as a LOVESWEPT author!

Touching and funny by turns, **THE MIDNIGHT SPECIAL,** LOVESWEPT #70, is another grand romance by Sara Orwig. As you know from her biographical sketch, Sara is a mother. But the four monster children who look like angels and behave like devils in her November LOVESWEPT romance come purely from the author's imagination. I've met Sara's lovely family and I can assure you that her own children do not bear the slightest resemblance to her hero's, Nick Bannon's, nephews! Those boys have sent more than a dozen teachers packing ... but they—and their uncle—have never met the likes of Maggie Linden! A determined beauty, Maggie prevails over mice in her suitcase and snakes in her bed. But her heart won't let her prevail over Nick. His pursuit is determined ... and delicious! **THE MIDNIGHT SPECIAL** is *very* special indeed ... another winner of a love story from Sara Orwig.

Do be sure to look in the back of this book for the excerpt from **HEARTS OF FIRE**, the latest historical from Christina Savage. I trust you'll find the teaser intriguing and that you'll be sure to ask your bookseller for the novel, coming to you from Bantam next month. Have a glorious November!

Warm wishes,

Carolyn Nichols

Carolyn Nichols
  Editor
LOVESWEPT
Bantam Books, Inc.
666 Fifth Avenue
New York, NY 10103

A special preview of

HEARTS
OF
FIRE

by Christina Savage
author of LOVE'S WILDEST FIRES

On sale November 1, 1984 wherever
Bantam paperbacks are sold

She was a Tryon and a lady, a proud, raven-tressed beauty from a great Philadelphia family divided by war—a family now driven to open conflict by notorious rebel Lucas Jericho, who challenged Cassie Tryon to love as never before. Dynamic, passionate opponents, soon they were swept away on a feverish tide . . . until family tragedy trapped Cassie between her Rebel lover and her loyalty to her Tory brother. As a patriot heiress in a Tory-occupied city, Cassie achingly surrendered her dreams of Lucas and his maddening touch. She would live dangerously, love recklessly, and command her father's mighty empire until she could reclaim the pirate prince torn from her arms by a brother's betrayal and the cruelties of war.

Turn the page for a dramatic excerpt from
HEARTS OF FIRE.

HEARTS OF FIRE

By Christina Savage

Cassie escaped into the tiny rear foyer and onto the porch. The garden, she saw instantly, was empty. Which was curious, she thought, descending the steps and looking around the corner of the house. She was certain Robal had said the rear garden, but there wasn't a soul in sight.

A joke? Not likely. Robal was noted for a total lack of humor. Unheeding of the shade and slight, cooling breeze, she hurried down the path of chipped rock and peered through the wrought-iron oak foliage of the rear gate. The drive, too, was empty. "Hello?" she called. "Louis?"

Silence was her only answer. Concerned, she stepped into the drive in time to hear a jangle of harness and see a horse and carriage emerge from the stable, the driver hidden in shadows. "What in heaven's name . . . ? Louis? Robal said—"

"My compliments." Lucas reined the mare to an abrupt halt in front of her. He leaned out of the carriage and offered her his hand. "C'mon up."

"But I . . . I can't," Cassie stammered, thrilled to see him and yet reluctant to obey. "I have guests. Robal said you were in the garden."

"I was, at the time. C'mon."

Common sense and social obligations would prevail if she hesitated. Before she could change her mind, she caught his hand and allowed herself to be pulled into the carriage.

"See here!" Louis shouted, running from the stable.

"Take care of my horse," Lucas called back over his shoulder. "She's had a long run. I expect her watered and fed by the time we get back. And rubbed down, too, Miss Tryon says."

Louis jerked off his cap and stared up at Cassie. "Sorry, miss," he gulped. "I didn't know . . . That is, I thought . . ."

"It's all right, Louis." Somehow, she managed to appear as if the whole episode had been planned. "Do as he says, please."

"But be careful," Lucas warned, sending the mare forward with a burst of speed that left Louis dodging a shower of gravel. "She bites."

"This is insane," Cassie said as they turned into the alley. "There must be fifty people back there who'll . . . Whatever will I tell them?"

"That you were kidnapped," Lucas said matter-of-factly.

"Oh, God, Lucas."

"Very well, then." He grinned, took her hand and tucked it in his arm. "Will rescued do?"

He was mad. But then, Cassie thought, so was she. And quite content to be so, under the circumstances.

The carriage rumbled down the alley, slowed for the turn onto Fourth Street, and left Jedediah's wake behind in the settling dust. They turned west on Walnut and drove the two and a half blocks to the entrance of South East Square. Seemingly misnamed—it lay to the southwest of the packed and bustling center of town—the park consisted of twenty carefully tended acres that served as a symbol of beauty and serenity in the midst of otherwise untrammeled growth. The land rose and fell in emerald swells whose sweep was broken by widely separated shade trees. In its center, protected by a ring of weeping willows, wild ducks and white swans glided tranquilly across a broad, deep blue pond that was adorned, at one end, with soft green lily pads and creamy white blossoms. Lucas steered the mare off the path and to a halt beneath a giant elm. "Walk?" he asked.

Cassie nodded her assent. "How did you hear . . . the news?"

Lucas jumped down and rounded the carriage. "My first mate returned from town this morning. I rode out immediately when I heard." He took Cassie's hands to help her down. "It's a hell of a thing."

"I hadn't thought of it in those terms," Cassie said with wry sarcasm, and then stopped short as her dress snagged in the bench seat's leaf spring. "Damn!" she cursed, falling against Lucas.

"Hang on. Let me see . . ." He held her with his left hand, reached around her with his right, and caught a provocative glimpse of ankle and calf. Almost suspended, she would fall if he let her go to free her skirt without damage, so he shrugged and gave a sharp jerk. The hem tore free, leaving a small piece behind. "Sorry," he said, still holding her though the need had passed.

Cassie caught up her skirt, inspected it, and let it drop. "It can be mended," she said with a sigh of resignation.

"But how about you?" Lucas asked. "Can you be mended?"

"I thought we were going to walk."

After four solid days of talk, the silence was blissful. No carriages arriving or leaving. No women chattering, no men deep in serious discussion. No questions, no solicitous comments to be acknowledged. Only the soft soughing of the wind in the trees, the occasional cry of a bird or chatter of a squirrel. Lucas walked at her side. The breeze ruffled his sunbleached, golden hair. His shirt was open to midchest, revealing a soft blanket of tight curls, starkly white against deeply tanned, bronze-colored skin. A broad black belt with a steel buckle shaped like a helmsman's wheel circled his waist. His nankeen breeches were cut tightly, almost too revealingly, and tucked into high-topped, soft black boots that were molded to his calves by a year's hard wear. More dashingly handsome than any of the dozens of other men she had seen in the past four days, he seemed not more piratical, but rather more natural and less ill at ease than he had in the scrivener's garb in which he'd arrived at Tryon Manor. "Is it that obvious, then?" she asked, almost painfully aware of his scrutiny.

"Your eyes betray you. You haven't been eating, I daresay. Haven't slept . . . and you've yet to have a good cry."

"Oh?" Cassie bridled. "And what makes a pirate—privateer, I beg your pardon—like yourself such an authority on tears?"

"I watched my mother being raped and wanted her to die and to be dead myself. I blamed myself, then and years later again when she walked into the sea. I have cared for Barnaby, and held his head in my arms so he wouldn't have to watch them hang our father, as I did." His voice was soft, as if lost somewhere in dreams or time. "I know about tears, Cassie. I'm an expert on tears. I am . . . an authority."

Cassie swallowed a knot in her throat. Her eyes burning, she fought her grief, tried desperately to push it back into the privacy of her heart. But so delicate a vessel was no match for her overwhelming sadness. "The Tryons . . . the Tryons are not given to tears," she gulped, and, as a great sob wracked her body, stopped and stood rigid and trembling.

"Come," Lucas said simply, leading her to the

willows. And there, hidden from the world by the soft green canopy of leaves, took her into his arms, dropped to his knees and to the ground, and held her like a babe.

The grass was cool, his arms around her and his body against her warm, a promise of safety. Society forbade her to be with a man like Lucas, but she no longer cared. In him was comfort; in him was safety. With him she needn't fear revealing her weakness. Slowly, the tension subsided and she relaxed and wept openly and unashamedly. She wept for her loss, for her loneliness. She wept for her fear and her uncertainty, for her father whom she had loved so deeply, and as all those who have known sorrow know so well, wept for herself.

Tears of anguish, tears of desolation. Hot and bitter tears that as they spilled, cleansed the soul of the poisons of excess grief. Lucas's hold was firm yet tender. His voice soothed her, and his arms gave her strength. One hand soothed her hair as her tears wet his chest. One emotion denied stifles all other emotions. The control over heart and head, the injunction not to feel, spreads. All is dulled until the door is opened and, so long pent up, a flood of emotion is released. Sometimes comes anger, sometimes fear, sometimes gratitude. Sometimes, too, comes a ravenous hunger for a contradiction of death and an affirmation of life, and even more a desire beyond all bounds to love and be loved. Blindly seeking him, Cassie found his lips, crushed her body to his, and breathed his name over and over again in her need to envelop his soul, to drink in his very being.

Lucas was at first taken aback, then swept along by the tide of her emotion. Pleasure overcoming surprise, he pressed her against the grass as his tongue slid along hers. His hands, roughly and then tenderly, caressed her sides, paused beneath the mounds of her breasts, moved gently to cup them for one brief, sweet second before continuing to the pale white of her throat and the string holding her bodice closed.

The kiss ended abruptly with the sound of laughter. Their eyes snapped open and their heads turned as one. "Oh, dear!" Cassie gasped, her voice lost under Lucas's heartfelt curse.

Two children, a boy and a girl of no more than ten years, stood peering between the draping branches of the willow. "Get out of here, you!" Lucas ordered.

The girl giggled.

Shoeless and dressed in homespun, the boy grabbed her hand and tugged at her. "C'mon, Beth."

Lucas jumped to his feet and feinted in their direction. "Go on. Git!" He added as the girl squealed in terror and the pair darted away.

Cassie rose shakily and smoothed her skirts.

"Damn kids," Lucas muttered. "Get underfoot when you least expect them—or want them."

"I think providence must've taken a hand," Cassie said, fiddling with her hair to hide her embarrassment. "What must you think of me?"

Lucas took her hands and kissed one and then the other. "None the worse, believe me. I think you're a remarkably brave young woman."

"Brazen, perhaps. Hardly brave." Her face and eyes felt puffy, but she counted that a small price to pay for the relief her tears had brought her. "We were going to walk, remember?" she asked, more kindly than before.

"All too well," Lucas admitted. He held out his arm for her to take, parted the screening branches so they could pass. "Mademoiselle?"

The land sloped gently toward the water's edge. As they approached, a mallard guided her half-grown brood to the safety of the far side of the pond. "I prayed you'd come, you know," Cassie said. "I was so lonely and frightened. Richard's been so distant, and Abigail and I don't get along at all. Jim is marvelous, as always, but I wanted to talk to you."

She smiled shyly up at him. "Do you think that terribly forward of me?"

"No." He turned, followed the water's edge. "I was thinking, when you were crying, how much I wished you'd been there to hold me when I cried."

Cassie squeezed his arm to her side. "I wish I had been too."

"I've learned something from this," he said softly. "If you find someone you trust . . . and love . . . enough to cry in front of, I've found the woman . . . that is, you've found the person you've been looking for, and you'd better not let her, or him, go."

Cassie stopped and turned to him. "Do you know what?" she asked, her fingers light on his cheek.

Lucas smiled. "What?"

"I think you're right. But—" she stretched up on tiptoe to kiss him fleetingly "—this is the wrong time and place, and since I don't trust myself, let's keep walking."

They rounded the end of the pond, startling a sleeping turtle into splashing flight. "You should have sent for me the moment it happened. Espey and Ullman knew where I was. An accident, wasn't it?"

Able at last to talk about her father's death with some degree of equanimity, Cassie recounted the events of the previous Saturday morning. "It's strange," she went on, "but I can't walk past his study without looking in and expecting him to be there and to tell me this has all been some macabre misunderstanding. A joke we'll laugh about as we sit around a winter fire."

It wasn't a joke. It was a calamity. The news of Jedediah's death had struck Lucas like a bombshell. Their agreement had been verbal, and it was a foregone conclusion that Richard, Jedediah's natural heir, wouldn't honor it, which meant he'd have to find a new investor before the end of the next week or face losing *The Sword of Guilford*. His one cause for hope had been an additional piece of information that could more properly be classified as a rumor. Billings, his first mate, had heard that the son had been cut off in favor of either the wife or the daughter. Grasping at this as a man overboard would have grasped a lifeline, Lucas saddled his mare and rode immediately and openly to Philadelphia.

He had been tempted to ask the moment he'd seen her, but had known that to do so would have been impolite. But as much as he loved her, as much as he sympathized with her grief and honestly tried to give her solace, the question had never been far from the tip of his tongue. An hour after his arrival, he was still burning with curiosity. "I won't be able to stay in town long," he said in an oblique approach to the all-important question. "I, ah, suppose you'll be living in town until Richard gets things sorted out?"

"Until Richard . . . ?" Cassie looked up at him quizzically and then understood. "Oh. No," she said, evidently troubled. "I'm afraid Richard won't be doing any sorting out."

Lucas's heart leaped, but he disguised his joy. "He won't? I don't understand."

"I mean Father cut Richard off. He left everything to me."

"It's true, then!" Lucas blurted without thinking. "Thank God!"

"I beg your pardon?" Cassie asked, unwilling to believe what she'd just heard. She stopped abruptly and stared up at him. "What did you just say?"

Lucas cursed mentally.

"You knew," Cassie went on accusingly.

"No," Lucas said, trying, too late, to explain. "Heard. A rumor. But it seemed like the wrong time to talk about . . ." He paused, threw up his hands. "The truth is, your father and I had an agreement, and I was afraid that if Richard had inherited everything, I'd be in danger of losing my ship."

"And just what did father promise you?" Cassie asked coldly.

There was nothing to be done but to continue and hope for the best. Haltingly at first, embarrassed by having been caught out, Lucas explained the terms of the agreement and the importance of receiving the money by the end of the next week.

"You couldn't have cared less," Cassie said sadly. "You didn't care about Father, didn't care about me—"

"That's not true," Lucas protested. "Asking a perfectly sensible question, under the circumstances, doesn't preclude caring."

"Caring for what?" Cassie snapped. "My money? So you can build your damned boat and sail around killing Englishmen? That's the reason you came rushing here so fast. The *only* reason. You were worried that your agreement with my father was buried with him."

"Cass—"

"And I played the fool, didn't I? The grieving daughter. Throw your strong arms around her. Tell her about your own tears. What was it? An expert on tears? An authority?" Her voice crackled with sarcasm and her eyes blazed with fury. "Tell me how brave I am? How bold? Well, what about how easily manipulated? What about gullible and trusting and . . . and . . ." Near tears again, she whirled and fled toward the carriage.

"Wait!" Lucas said, catching up with her and grabbing her arm. "I meant nothing of the sort and you know it. You're not being fair, damn it."

"Not being fair?" Cassie asked with exaggerated sweetness that only emphasized her anger. "Why, of course I'll be fair, Lucas. You needn't worry about that. I'll see my father's bargain through. You'll get your money, sir, and your cursed boat." She stared at his hand until he loosed her arm, then into his eyes. "And now"—the sweetness became acid strong enough to etch glass—"I should like to be taken home, if you don't mind. I trust you are gentleman enough not to refuse."

Lucas sighed. "All right, Cassie," he said, stepping out of her way. "Whatever you say."

"Exactly," Cassie hissed, and with a contemptuous toss of her head, she stalked past him.

A dozen expletives flashed through his mind, but none of them seemed appropriate. Lucas stared down at his reflection on the surface of the pond. A water- wind-rippled privateer stared back. He stooped down, picked up a stone, and threw it into his likeness, then wheeled around in disgust and started after Cassie.

A TRIUMPHANT NOVEL
BY THE AUTHOR OF
THE PROUD BREED

WILD SWAN

Celeste De Blasis

Spanning decades and sweeping from England's West Country in the years of the Napoleonic Wars to the beauty of Maryland's horse country—a golden land shadowed by slavery and soon to be ravaged by war—here is a novel richly spun of authentically detailed history and sumptuous romance, a rewarding woman's story in the grand tradition of A WOMAN OF SUBSTANCE. WILD SWAN is the story of Alexandria Thaine, youngest and unwanted child of a bitter mother and distant father— suddenly summoned home to care for her dead sister's children. Alexandria—for whom the brief joys of childhood are swiftly forgotten . . . and the bright fire of passion nearly extinguished.

Buy WILD SWAN, on sale in hardcover August 15, 1984, wherever Bantam Books are sold, or use the handy coupon below for ordering:

LOVESWEPT

Love Stories you'll never forget by authors you'll always remember

☐	21603	**Heaven's Price #1** Sandra Brown	$1.95
☐	21604	**Surrender #2** Helen Mittermeyer	$1.95
☐	21600	**The Joining Stone #3** Noelle Berry McCue	$1.95
☐	21601	**Silver Miracles #4** Fayrene Preston	$1.95
☐	21605	**Matching Wits #5** Carla Neggers	$1.95
☐	21606	**A Love for All Time #6** Dorothy Garlock	$1.95
☐	21607	**A Tryst With Mr. Lincoln? #7** Billie Green	$1.95
☐	21602	**Temptation's Sting #8** Helen Conrad	$1.95
☐	21608	**December 32nd . . . And Always #9** Marie Michael	$1.95
☐	21609	**Hard Drivin' Man #10** Nancy Carlson	$1.95
☐	21610	**Beloved Intruder #11** Noelle Berry McCue	$1.95
☐	21611	**Hunter's Payne #12** Joan J. Domning	$1.95
☐	21618	**Tiger Lady #13** Joan Domning	$1.95
☐	21613	**Stormy Vows #14** Iris Johansen	$1.95
☐	21614	**Brief Delight #15** Helen Mittermeyer	$1.95
☐	21616	**A Very Reluctant Knight #16** Billie Green	$1.95
☐	21617	**Tempest at Sea #17** Iris Johansen	$1.95
☐	21619	**Autumn Flames #18** Sara Orwig	$1.95
☐	21620	**Pfarr Lake Affair #19** Joan Domning	$1.95
☐	21621	**Heart on a String #20** Carla Neggars	$1.95
☐	21622	**The Seduction of Jason #21** Fayrene Preston	$1.95
☐	21623	**Breakfast In Bed #22** Sandra Brown	$1.95
☐	21624	**Taking Savannah #23** Becky Combs	$1.95
☐	21625	**The Reluctant Lark #24** Iris Johansen	$1.95

Prices and availability subject to change without notice.

Buy them at your local bookstore or use this handy coupon for ordering:

Bantam Books, Inc., Dept. SW, 414 East Golf Road, Des Plaines, Ill. 60016

Please send me the books I have checked above. I am enclosing $_____ (please add $1.25 to cover postage and handling). Send check or money order—no cash or C.O.D.'s please.

Mr/Ms_____

Address _____

City/State_____ Zip_____

SW—9/84

Please allow four to six weeks for delivery. This offer expires 3/85.

LOVESWEPT

Love Stories you'll never forget by authors you'll always remember

Prices and availability subject to change without notice.

Buy them at your local bookstore or use this handy coupon for ordering:

LOVESWEPT

*Love Stories you'll never forget
by authors you'll always remember*

Prices and availability subject to change without notice.

Buy them at your local bookstore or use this handy coupon for ordering: